The God of His Fathers
Tales of the Klondyke

Jack London

The God of His Fathers: Tales of the Klondyke

Copyright © 2018 Bibliotech Press
All rights reserved

ISBN: 978-1-61895-371-1

These tales have appeared in "McClure's," "Ainslee's," "Outing," the "Overland Monthly," the "Wave," the "National," and the San Francisco "Examiner." To the kindness of the various editors is due their reappearance in more permanent form.

TO THE DAUGHTERS OF THE WOLF WHO HAVE BRED
AND SUCKLED A RACE OF MEN

CONTENTS

THE GOD OF HIS FATHERS

I

On every hand stretched the forest primeval,—the home of noisy comedy and silent tragedy. Here the struggle for survival continued to wage with all its ancient brutality. Briton and Russian were still to overlap in the Land of the Rainbow's End—and this was the very heart of it—nor had Yankee gold yet purchased its vast domain. The wolf-pack still clung to the flank of the cariboo-herd, singling out the weak and the big with calf, and pulling them down as remorselessly as were it a thousand, thousand generations into the past. The sparse aborigines still acknowledged the rule of their chiefs and medicine men, drove out bad spirits, burned their witches, fought their neighbors, and ate their enemies with a relish which spoke well of their bellies. But it was at the moment when the stone age was drawing to a close. Already, over unknown trails and chartless wildernesses, were the harbingers of the steel arriving,—fair-faced, blue-eyed, indomitable men, incarnations of the unrest of their race. By accident or design, single-handed and in twos and threes, they came from no one knew whither, and fought, or died, or passed on, no one knew whence. The priests raged against them, the chiefs called forth their fighting men, and stone clashed with steel; but to little purpose. Like water seeping from some mighty reservoir, they trickled through the dark forests and mountain passes, threading the highways in bark canoes, or with their moccasined feet breaking trail for the wolf-dogs. They came of a great breed, and their mothers were many; but the fur-clad denizens of the Northland had this yet to learn. So many an unsung wanderer fought his last and died under the cold fire of the aurora, as did his brothers in burning sands and reeking jungles, and as they shall

1

continue to do till in the fulness of time the destiny of their race be achieved.

It was near twelve. Along the northern horizon a rosy glow, fading to the west and deepening to the east, marked the unseen dip of the midnight sun. The gloaming and the dawn were so commingled that there was no night,—simply a wedding of day with day, a scarcely perceptible blending of two circles of the sun. A kildee timidly chirped good-night; the full, rich throat of a robin proclaimed good-morrow. From an island on the breast of the Yukon a colony of wild fowl voiced its interminable wrongs, while a loon laughed mockingly back across a still stretch of river.

In the foreground, against the bank of a lazy eddy, birch-bark canoes were lined two and three deep. Ivory-bladed spears, bone-barbed arrows, buckskin-thonged bows, and simple basket-woven traps bespoke the fact that in the muddy current of the river the salmon-run was on. In the background, from the tangle of skin tents and drying frames, rose the voices of the fisher folk. Bucks skylarked with bucks or flirted with the maidens, while the older squaws, shut out from this by virtue of having fulfilled the end of their existence in reproduction, gossiped as they braided rope from the green roots of trailing vines. At their feet their naked progeny played and squabbled, or rolled in the muck with the tawny wolf-dogs.

To one side of the encampment, and conspicuously apart from it, stood a second camp of two tents. But it was a white man's camp. If nothing else, the choice of position at least bore convincing evidence of this. In case of offence, it commanded the Indian quarters a hundred yards away; of defense, a rise to the ground and the cleared intervening space; and last, of defeat, the swift slope of a score of yards to the canoes below. From one of the tents came the petulant cry of a sick child and the crooning song of a mother. In the open, over the smoldering embers of a fire, two men held talk.

2

"Eh? I love the church like a good son. *Bien!* So great a love that my days have been spent in fleeing away from her, and my nights in dreaming dreams of reckoning. Look you!" The half-breed's voice rose to an angry snarl. "I am Red River born. My father was white—as white as you. But you are Yankee, and he was British bred, and a gentleman's son. And my mother was the daughter of a chief, and I was a man. Ay, and one had to look the second time to see what manner of blood ran in my veins; for I lived with the whites, and was one of them, and my father's heart beat in me. It happened there was a maiden—white—who looked on me with kind eyes. Her father had much land and many horses; also he was a big man among his people, and his blood was the blood of the French. He said the girl knew not her own mind, and talked overmuch with her, and became wroth that such things should be.

"But she knew her mind, for we came quick before the priest. And quicker had come her father, with lying words, false promises, I know not what; so that the priest stiffened his neck and would not make us that we might live one with the other. As at the beginning it was the church which would not bless my birth, so now it was the church which refused me marriage and put the blood of men upon my hands. *Bien!* Thus have I cause to love the church. So I struck the priest on his woman's mouth, and we took swift horses, the girl and I, to Fort Pierre, where was a minister of good heart. But hot on our trail was her father, and brothers, and other men he had gathered to him. And we fought, our horses on the run, till I emptied three saddles and the rest drew off and went on to Fort Pierre. Then we took east, the girl and I, to the hills and forests, and we lived one with the other, and we were not married,—the work of the good church which I love like a son.

"But mark you, for this is the strangeness of woman, the way of which no man may understand. One of the saddles I emptied was that of her father's, and the hoofs of those who came behind had pounded him into the earth. This we saw, the girl and I, and this I had forgot had she not remembered.

3

And in the quiet of the evening, after the day's hunt were done, it came between us, and in the silence of the night when we lay beneath the stars and should have been one. It was there always. She never spoke, but it sat by our fire and held us ever apart. She tried to put it aside, but at such times it would rise up till I could read it in the look of her eyes, in the very intake of her breath.

"So in the end she bore me a child, a woman-child, and died. Then I went among my mother's people, that it might nurse at a warm breast and live. But my hands were wet with the blood of men, look you, because of the church, wet with the blood of men. And the Riders of the North came for me, but my mother's brother, who was then chief in his own right, hid me and gave me horses and food. And we went away, my woman-child and I, even to the Hudson Bay Country, where white men were few and the questions they asked not many. And I worked for the company a hunter, as a guide, as a driver of dogs, till my woman-child was become a woman, tall, and slender, and fair to the eye.

"You know the winter, long and lonely, breeding evil thoughts and bad deeds. The Chief Factor was a hard man, and bold. And he was not such that a woman would delight in looking upon. But he cast eyes upon my woman-child who was become a woman. Mother of God! he sent me away on a long trip with the dogs, that he might—you understand, he was a hard man and without heart. She was most white, and her soul was white, and a good woman, and—well, she died.

"It was bitter cold the night of my return, and I had been away months, and the dogs were limping sore when I came to the fort. The Indians and breeds looked on me in silence, and I felt the fear of I knew not what, but I said nothing till the dogs were fed and I had eaten as a man with work before him should. Then I spoke up, demanding the word, and they shrank from me, afraid of my anger and what I should do; but the story came out, the pitiful story, word for word and act for act, and they marveled that I should be so quiet.

4

"When they had done I went to the Factor's house, calmer than now in the telling of it. He had been afraid and called upon the breeds to help him; but they were not pleased with the deed, and had left him to lie on the bed he had made. So he had fled to the house of the priest. Thither I followed. But when I was come to that place, the priest stood in my way, and spoke soft words, and said a man in anger should go neither to the right nor left, but straight to God. I asked by the right of a father's wrath that he give me past, but he said only over his body, and besought with me to pray. Look you, it was the church, always the church; for I passed over his body and sent the Factor to meet my woman-child before his god, which is a bad god, and the god of the white men.

"Then was there hue and cry, for word was sent to the station below, and I came away. Through the Land of the Great Slave, down the Valley of the Mackenzie to the never-opening ice, over the White Rockies, past the Great Curve of the Yukon, even to this place did I come. And from that day to this, yours is the first face of my father's people I have looked upon. May it be the last! These people, which are my people, are a simple folk, and I have been raised to honor among them. My word is their law, and their priests but do my bidding, else would I not suffer them. When I speak for them I speak for myself. We ask to be let alone. We do not want your kind. If we permit you to sit by our fires, after you will come your church, your priests, and your gods. And know this, for each white man who comes to my village, him will I make deny his god. You are the first, and I give you grace. So it were well you go, and go quickly."

"I am not responsible for my brothers," the second man spoke up, filling his pipe in a meditative manner. Hay Stockard was at times as thoughtful of speech as he was wanton of action; but only at times.

"But I know your breed," responded the other. "Your brothers are many, and it is you and yours who break the trail for them to follow. In time they shall come to possess the land,

5

but not in my time. Already, have I heard, are they on the head-reaches of the Great River, and far away below are the Russians."

Hay Stockard lifted his head with a quick start. This was startling geographical information. The Hudson Bay post at Fort Yukon had other notions concerning the course of the river, believing it to flow into the Arctic.

"Then the Yukon empties into Bering Sea?" he asked.

"I do not know, but below there are Russians, many Russians. Which is neither here nor there. You may go on and see for yourself; you may go back to your brothers; but up the Koyukuk you shall not go while the priests and fighting men do my bidding. Thus do I command, I, Baptiste the Red, whose word is law and who am head man over this people."

"And should I not go down to the Russians, or back to my brothers?"

"Then shall you go swift-footed before your god, which is a bad god, and the god of the white men."

The red sun shot up above the northern sky-line, dripping and bloody. Baptiste the Red came to his feet, nodded curtly, and went back to his camp amid the crimson shadows and the singing of the robins.

Hay Stockard finished his pipe by the fire, picturing in smoke and coal the unknown upper reaches of the Koyukuk, the strange stream which ended here its arctic travels and merged its waters with the muddy Yukon flood. Somewhere up there, if the dying words of a ship-wrecked sailorman who had made the fearful overland journey were to be believed, and if the vial of golden grains in his pouch attested anything,—somewhere up there, in that home of winter, stood the Treasure House of the North. And as keeper of the gate, Baptiste the Red, English half-breed and renegade, barred the way.

"Bah!" He kicked the embers apart and rose to his full height, arms lazily outstretched, facing the flushing north with careless soul.

II

Hay Stockard swore, harshly, in the rugged monosyllables of his mother tongue. His wife lifted her gaze from the pots and pans, and followed his in a keen scrutiny of the river. She was a woman of the Teslin Country, wise in the ways of her husband's vernacular when it grew intensive. From the slipping of a snow-shoe thong to the forefront of sudden death, she could gauge occasion by the pitch and volume of his blasphemy. So she knew the present occasion merited attention. A long canoe, with paddles flashing back the rays of the westering sun, was crossing the current from above and urging in for the eddy. Hay Stockard watched it intently. Three men rose and dipped, rose and dipped, in rhythmical precision; but a red bandanna, wrapped about the head of one, caught and held his eye.

"Bill!" he called. "Oh, Bill!"

A shambling, loose-jointed giant rolled out of one of the tents, yawning and rubbing the sleep from his eyes. Then he sighted the strange canoe and was wide awake on the instant.

"By the jumping Methuselah! That damned sky-pilot!"

Hay Stockard nodded his head bitterly, half-reached for his rifle, then shrugged his shoulders.

"Pot-shot him," Bill suggested, "and settle the thing out of hand. He'll spoil us sure if we don't." But the other declined this drastic measure and turned away, at the same time bidding the woman return to her work, and calling Bill back

7

from the bank. The two Indians in the canoe moored it on the edge of the eddy, while its white occupant, conspicuous by his gorgeous head-gear, came up the bank.

"Like Paul of Tarsus, I give you greeting. Peace be unto you and grace before the Lord."

His advances were met sullenly, and without speech.

"To you, Hay Stockard, blasphemer and Philistine, greeting. In your heart is the lust of Mammon, in your mind cunning devils, in your tent this woman whom you live with in adultery; yet of these divers sins, even here in the wilderness, I, Sturges Owen, apostle to the Lord, bid you to repent and cast from you your iniquities."

"Save your cant! Save your cant!" Hay Stockard broke in testily. "You'll need all you've got, and more, for Red Baptiste over yonder."

He waved his hand toward the Indian camp, where the half-breed was looking steadily across, striving to make out the newcomers. Sturges Owen, disseminator of light and apostle to the Lord, stepped to the edge of the steep and commanded his men to bring up the camp outfit. Stockard followed him.

"Look here," he demanded, plucking the missionary by the shoulder and twirling him about. "Do you value your hide?"

"My life is in the Lord's keeping, and I do but work in His vineyard," he replied solemnly.

"Oh, stow that! Are you looking for a job of martyrship?"

"If He so wills."

"Well, you'll find it right here, but I'm going to give you some advice first. Take it or leave it. If you stop here, you'll be cut off in the midst of your labors. And not you alone, but your men, Bill, my wife—"

8

"Who is a daughter of Belial and hearkeneth not to the true Gospel."

"And myself. Not only do you bring trouble upon yourself, but upon us. I was frozen in with you last winter, as you will well recollect, and I know you for a good man and a fool. If you think it your duty to strive with the heathen, well and good; but, do exercise some wit in the way you go about it. This man, Red Baptiste, is no Indian. He comes of our common stock, is as bull-necked as I ever dared be, and as wild a fanatic the one way as you are the other. When you two come together, hell'll be to pay, and I don't care to be mixed up in it. Understand? So take my advice and go away. If you go down-stream, you'll fall in with the Russians. There's bound to be Greek priests among them, and they'll see you safe through to Bering Sea,—that's where the Yukon empties,—and from there it won't be hard to get back to civilization. Take my word for it and get out of here as fast as God'll let you."

"He who carries the Lord in his heart and the Gospel in his hand hath no fear of the machinations of man or devil," the missionary answered stoutly. "I will see this man and wrestle with him. One backslider returned to the fold is a greater victory than a thousand heathen. He who is strong for evil can be as mighty for good, witness Saul when he journeyed up to Damascus to bring Christian captives to Jerusalem. And the voice of the Savior came to him, crying, 'Saul, Saul, why persecutest thou me?' And therewith Paul arrayed himself on the side of the Lord, and thereafter was most mighty in the saving of souls. And even as thou, Paul of Tarsus, even so do I work in the vineyard of the Lord, bearing trials and tribulations, scoffs and sneers, stripes and punishments, for His dear sake."

"Bring up the little bag with the tea and a kettle of water," he called the next instant to his boatmen; "not forgetting the haunch of caribou and the mixing-pan."

When his men, converts by his own hand, had gained the

bank, the trio fell to their knees, hands and backs burdened with camp equipage, and offered up thanks for their passage through the wilderness and their safe arrival. Hay Stockard looked upon the function with sneering disapproval, the romance and solemnity of it lost to his matter-of-fact soul. Baptiste the Red, still gazing across, recognized the familiar postures, and remembered the girl who had shared his star-roofed couch in the hills and forests, and the woman-child who lay somewhere by bleak Hudson's Bay.

III

"Confound it, Baptiste, couldn't think of it. Not for a moment. Grant that this man is a fool and of small use in the nature of things, but still, you know, I can't give him up."

Hay Stockard paused, striving to put into speech the rude ethics of his heart.

"He's worried me, Baptiste, in the past and now, and caused me all manner of troubles; but can't you see, he's my own breed—white—and—and—why, I couldn't buy my life with his, not if he was a nigger."

"So be it," Baptiste the Red made answer. "I have given you grace and choice. I shall come presently, with my priests and fighting men, and either shall I kill you, or you deny your god. Give up the priest to my pleasure, and you shall depart in peace. Otherwise your trail ends here. My people are against you to the babies. Even now have the children stolen away your canoes." He pointed down to the river. Naked boys had slipped down the water from the point above, cast loose the canoes, and by then had worked them into the current. When they had drifted out of rifle-shot they clambered over the sides and paddled ashore.

"Give me the priest, and you may have them back again. Come! Speak your mind, but without haste."

Stockard shook his head. His glance dropped to the woman

10

of the Teslin Country with his boy at her breast, and he would have wavered had he not lifted his eyes to the men before him.

"I am not afraid," Sturges Owen spoke up. "The Lord bears me in his right hand, and alone am I ready to go into the camp of the unbeliever. It is not too late. Faith may move mountains. Even in the eleventh hour may I win his soul to the true righteousness."

"Trip the beggar up and make him fast," Bill whispered hoarsely in the ear of his leader, while the missionary kept the floor and wrestled with the heathen. "Make him hostage, and bore him if they get ugly."

"No," Stockard answered. "I gave him my word that he could speak with us unmolested. Rules of warfare, Bill; rules of warfare. He's been on the square, given us warning, and all that, and—why, damn it, man, I can't break my word!"

"He'll keep his, never fear."

"Don't doubt it, but I won't let a half-breed outdo me in fair dealing. Why not do what he wants,—give him the missionary and be done with it?"

"N-no," Bill hesitated doubtfully.

"Shoe pinches, eh?"

Bill flushed a little and dropped the discussion. Baptiste the Red was still waiting the final decision. Stockard went up to him.

"It's this way, Baptiste. I came to your village minded to go up the Koyukuk. I intended no wrong. My heart was clean of evil. It is still clean. Along comes this priest, as you call him. I didn't bring him here. He'd have come whether I was here or not. But now that he is here, being of my people, I've got to stand by him. And I'm going to. Further, it will be no

11

child's play. When you have done, your village will be silent and empty, your people wasted as after a famine. True, we will he gone; likewise the pick of your fighting men—"

"But those who remain shall be in peace, nor shall the word of strange gods and the tongues of strange priests be buzzing in their ears."

Both men shrugged their shoulder and turned away, the half-breed going back to his own camp. The missionary called his two men to him, and they fell into prayer. Stockard and Bill attacked the few standing pines with their axes, felling them into convenient breastworks. The child had fallen asleep, so the woman placed it on a heap of furs and lent a hand in fortifying the camp. Three sides were thus defended, the steep declivity at the rear precluding attack from that direction. When these arrangements had been completed, the two men stalked into the open, clearing away, here and there, the scattered underbrush. From the opposing camp came the booming of war-drums and the voices of the priests stirring the people to anger.

"Worst of it is they'll come in rushes," Bill complained as they walked back with shouldered axes.

"And wait till midnight, when the light gets dim for shooting."

"Can't start the ball a-rolling too early, then." Bill exchanged the axe for a rifle, and took a careful rest. One of the medicine-men, towering above his tribesmen, stood out distinctly. Bill drew a bead on him.

"All ready?" he asked.

Stockard opened the ammunition box, placed the woman where she could reload in safety, and gave the word. The medicine-man dropped. For a moment there was silence, then a wild howl went up and a flight of bone arrows fell short.

"I'd like to take a look at the beggar," Bill remarked, throwing a fresh shell into place. "I'll swear I drilled him clean between the eyes."

"Didn't work." Stockard shook his head gloomily. Baptiste had evidently quelled the more warlike of his followers, and instead of precipitating an attack in the bright light of day, the shot had caused a hasty exodus, the Indians drawing out of the village beyond the zone of fire.

In the full tide of his proselyting fervor, borne along by the hand of God, Sturges Owen would have ventured alone into the camp of the unbeliever, equally prepared for miracle or martyrdom; but in the waiting which ensued, the fever of conviction died away gradually, as the natural man asserted itself. Physical fear replaced spiritual hope; the love of life, the love of God. It was no new experience. He could feel his weakness coming on, and knew it of old time. He had struggled against it and been overcome by it before. He remembered when the other men had driven their paddles like mad in the van of a roaring ice-flood, how, at the critical moment, in a panic of worldly terror, he had dropped his paddle and besought wildly with his God for pity. And there were other times. The recollection was not pleasant. It brought shame to him that his spirit should be so weak and his flesh so strong. But the love of life! the love of life! He could not strip it from him. Because of it had his dim ancestors perpetuated their line; because of it was he destined to perpetuate his. His courage, if courage it might be called, was bred of fanaticism. The courage of Stockard and Bill was the adherence to deep-rooted ideals. Not that the love of life was less, but the love of race tradition more; not that they were unafraid to die, but that they were brave enough not to live at the price of shame.

The missionary rose, for the moment swayed by the mood of sacrifice. He half crawled over the barricade to proceed to the other camp, but sank back, a trembling mass, wailing: "As the spirit moves! As the spirit moves! Who am I that I should set aside the judgments of God? Before the

13

foundations of the world were all things written in the book of life. Worm that I am, shall I erase the page or any portion thereof? As God wills, so shall the spirit move!"

Bill reached over, plucked him to his feet, and shook him, fiercely, silently. Then he dropped the bundle of quivering nerves and turned his attention to the two converts. But they showed little fright and a cheerful alacrity in preparing for the coming passage at arms.

Stockard, who had been talking in undertones with the Teslin woman, now turned to the missionary.

"Fetch him over here," he commanded of Bill.

"Now," he ordered, when Sturges Owen had been duly deposited before him, "make us man and wife, and be lively about it." Then he added apologetically to Bill: "No telling how it's to end, so I just thought I'd get my affairs straightened up."

The woman obeyed the behest of her white lord. To her the ceremony was meaningless. By her lights she was his wife, and had been from the day they first foregathered. The converts served as witnesses. Bill stood over the missionary, prompting him when he stumbled. Stockard put the responses in the woman's mouth, and when the time came, for want of better, ringed her finger with thumb and forefinger of his own.

"Kiss the bride!" Bill thundered, and Sturges Owen was too weak to disobey.

"Now baptize the child!"

"Neat and tidy," Bill commented.

"Gathering the proper outfit for a new trail," the father explained, taking the boy from the mother's arms. "I was grub-staked, once, into the Cascades, and had everything in the kit except salt. Never shall forget it. And if the woman and the kid cross the divide to-night they might as well be prepared for pot-luck. A long shot, Bill, between ourselves, but nothing lost if it misses."

A cup of water served the purpose, and the child was laid away in a secure corner of the barricade. The men built the fire, and the evening meal was cooked.

The sun hurried round to the north, sinking closer to the horizon. The heavens in that quarter grew red and bloody. The shadows lengthened, the light dimmed, and in the somber recesses of the forest life slowly died away. Even the wild fowl in the river softened their raucous chatter and feigned the nightly farce of going to bed. Only the tribesmen increased their clamor, war-drums booming and voices raised in savage folk songs. But as the sun dipped they ceased their tumult. The rounded hush of midnight was complete. Stockard rose to his knees and peered over the logs. Once the child wailed in pain and disconcerted him. The mother bent over it, but it slept again. The silence was interminable, profound. Then, of a sudden, the robins burst into full-throated song. The night had passed.

A flood of dark figures boiled across the open. Arrows whistled and bow-thongs sang. The shrill-tongued rifles answered back. A spear, and a mighty cast, transfixed the Teslin woman as she hovered above the child. A spent arrow, diving between the logs, lodged in the missionary's arm.

There was no stopping the rush. The middle distance was cumbered with bodies, but the rest surged on, breaking against and over the barricade like an ocean wave. Sturges Owen fled to the tent, while the men were swept from their feet, buried beneath the human tide. Hay Stockard alone regained the surface, flinging the tribesmen aside like yelping curs. He had managed to seize an axe. A dark hand grasped the child by a naked foot, and drew it from beneath its mother. At arm's length its puny body circled through the

15

air, dashing to death against the logs. Stockard clove the man to the chin and fell to clearing space. The ring of savage faces closed in, raining upon him spear-thrusts and bone-barbed arrows. The sun shot up, and they swayed back and forth in the crimson shadows. Twice, with his axe blocked by too deep a blow, they rushed him; but each time he flung them clear. They fell underfoot and he trampled dead and dying, the way slippery with blood. And still the day brightened and the robins sang. Then they drew back from him in awe, and he leaned breathless upon his axe.

"Blood of my soul!" cried Baptiste the Red. "But thou art a man. Deny thy god, and thou shalt yet live."

Stockard swore his refusal, feebly but with grace.

"Behold! A woman!" Sturges Owen had been brought before the half-breed.

Beyond a scratch on the arm, he was uninjured, but his eyes roved about him in an ecstasy of fear. The heroic figure of the blasphemer, bristling with wounds and arrows, leaning defiantly upon his axe, indifferent, indomitable, superb, caught his wavering vision. And he felt a great envy of the man who could go down serenely to the dark gates of death. Surely Christ, and not he, Sturges Owen, had been molded in such manner. And why not he? He felt dimly the curse of ancestry, the feebleness of spirit which had come down to him out of the past, and he felt an anger at the creative force, symbolize it as he would, which had formed him, its servant, so weakly. For even a stronger man, this anger and the stress of circumstance were sufficient to breed apostasy, and for Sturges Owen it was inevitable. In the fear of man's anger he would dare the wrath of God. He had been raised up to serve the Lord only that he might be cast down. He had been given faith without the strength of faith; he had been given spirit without the power of spirit. It was unjust.

"Where now is thy god?" the half-breed demanded.

16

"I do not know." He stood straight and rigid, like a child repeating a catechism.

"Hast thou then a god at all?"

"I had."
"And now?"
"No."

Hay Stockard swept the blood from his eyes and laughed. The missionary looked at him curiously, as in a dream. A feeling of infinite distance came over him, as though of a great remove. In that which had transpired, and which was to transpire, he had no part. He was a spectator—at a distance, yes, at a distance. The words of Baptiste came to him faintly:-

"Very good. See that this man go free, and that no harm befall him. Let him depart in peace. Give him a canoe and food. Set his face toward the Russians, that he may tell their priests of Baptiste the Red, in whose country there is no god."

They led him to the edge of the steep, where they paused to witness the final tragedy. The half-breed turned to Hay Stockard.

"There is no god," he prompted.

The man laughed in reply. One of the young men poised a war-spear for the cast.

"Hast thou a god?"

"Ay, the God of my fathers."

He shifted the axe for a better grip. Baptiste the Red gave the sign, and the spear hurtled full against his breast. Sturges Owen saw the ivory head stand out beyond his back, saw the man sway, laughing, and snap the shaft short as he fell upon it. Then he went down to the river, that he might carry to the Russians the message of Baptiste the Red, in whose country there was no god.

THE GREAT INTERROGATION

I

To say the least, Mrs. Sayther's career in Dawson was meteoric. She arrived in the spring, with dog sleds and French-Canadian *voyageurs*, blazed gloriously for a brief month, and departed up the river as soon as it was free of ice. Now womanless Dawson never quite understood this hurried departure, and the local Four Hundred felt aggrieved and lonely till the Nome strike was made and old sensations gave way to new. For it had delighted in Mrs. Sayther, and received her wide-armed. She was pretty, charming, and, moreover, a widow. And because of this she at once had at heel any number of Eldorado Kings, officials, and adventuring younger sons, whose ears were yearning for the frou-frou of a woman's skirts.

The mining engineers revered the memory of her husband, the late Colonel Sayther, while the syndicate and promoter representatives spoke awesomely of his deals and manipulations; for he was known down in the States as a great mining man, and as even a greater one in London. Why his widow, of all women, should have come into the country, was the great interrogation. But they were a practical breed, the men of the Northland, with a wholesome disregard for theories and a firm grip on facts. And to not a few of them Karen Sayther was a most essential fact. That she did not regard the matter in this light, is evidenced by the neatness and celerity with which refusal and proposal tallied off during her four weeks' stay. And with her vanished the fact, and only the interrogation remained.

To the solution, Chance vouchsafed one clew. Her last victim, Jack Coughran, having fruitlessly laid at her feet both his heart and a five-hundred-foot creek claim on Bonanza, celebrated the misfortune by walking all of a night with the gods. In the midwatch of this night he happened to rub shoulders with Pierre Fontaine, none other than head man of Karen Sayther's *voyageurs*. This rubbing of shoulders led to recognition and drinks, and ultimately involved both men in a common muddle of inebriety.

"Heh?" Pierre Fontaine later on gurgled thickly. "Vot for Madame Sayther mak visitation to thees country? More better you spik wit her. I know no t'ing 'tall, only all de tam her ask one man's name. 'Pierre,' her spik wit me; 'Pierre, you moos' find thees mans, and I gif you mooch—one thousand dollar you find thees mans.' Thees mans? Ah, *oui*. Thees man's name—vot you call—Daveed Payne. *Oui*, m'sieu, Daveed Payne. All de tam her spik das name. And all de tam I look rount vaire mooch, work lak hell, but no can find das dam mans, and no get one thousand dollar 'tall. By dam!

"Heh? Ah, *oui*. One tam dose mens vot come from Circle City, dose mens know thees mans. Him Birch Creek, dey spik. And madame? Her say '*Bon!*' and look happy lak anyt'ing. And her spik wit me. 'Pierre,' her spik, 'harness de dogs. We go queek. We find thees mans I gif you one thousand dollar more.' And I say, '*Oui*, queek! *Allons, madame!*'

"For sure, I t'ink, das two thousand dollar mine. Bully boy! Den more mens come from Circle City, and dey say no, das thees mans, Daveed Payne, come Dawson leel tam back. So madame and I go not 'tall.

"*Oui, m'sieu.* Thees day madame spik. 'Pierre,' her spik, and gif me five hundred dollar, 'go buy poling-boat. To-morrow we go up de river.' Ah, *oui*, to-morrow, up de river, and das dam Sitka Charley mak me pay for de poling-boat five hundred dollar. Dam!"

Thus it was, when Jack Coughran unburdened himself next

day, that Dawson fell to wondering who was this David Payne, and in what way his existence bore upon Karen Sayther's. But that very day, as Pierre Fontaine had said, Mrs. Sayther and her barbaric crew of *voyageurs* towed up the east bank to Klondike City, shot across to the west bank to escape the bluffs, and disappeared amid the maze of islands to the south.

II

"*Oui, madame*, thees is de place. One, two, t'ree island below Stuart River. Thees is t'ree island."

As he spoke, Pierre Fontaine drove his pole against the bank and held the stern of the boat against the current. This thrust the bow in, till a nimble breed climbed ashore with the painter and made fast.

"One leel tam, madame, I go look see."

A chorus of dogs marked his disappearance over the edge of the bank, but a minute later he was back again.

"*Oui, madame*, thees is de cabin. I mak investigation. No can find mans at home. But him no go vaire far, vaire long, or him no leave dogs. Him come queek, you bet!"

"Help me out, Pierre. I'm tired all over from the boat. You might have made it softer, you know."

From a nest of furs amidships, Karen Sayther rose to her full height of slender fairness. But if she looked lily-frail in her elemental environment, she was belied by the grip she put upon Pierre's hand, by the knotting of her woman's biceps as it took the weight of her body, by the splendid effort of her limbs as they held her out from the perpendicular bank while she made the ascent. Though shapely flesh clothed delicate frame, her body was a seat of strength.

Still, for all the careless ease with which she had made the

21

landing, there was a warmer color than usual to her face, and a perceptibly extra beat to her heart. But then, also, it was with a certain reverent curiousness that she approached the cabin, while the Hush on her cheek showed a yet riper mellowness.

"Look, see!" Pierre pointed to the scattered chips by the woodpile. "Him fresh—two, t'ree day, no more."

Mrs. Sayther nodded. She tried to peer through the small window, but it was made of greased parchment which admitted light while it blocked vision. Failing this, she went round to the door, half lifted the rude latch to enter, but changed her mind and let it fall back into place. Then she suddenly dropped on one knee and kissed the rough-hewn threshold. If Pierre Fontaine saw, he gave no sign, and the memory in the time to come was never shared. But the next instant, one of the boatmen, placidly lighting his pipe, was startled by an unwonted harshness in his captain's voice.

"Hey! You! Le Goire! You mak'm soft more better," Pierre commanded. "Plenty bearskin; plenty blanket. Dam!"

But the nest was soon after disrupted, and the major portion tossed up to the crest of the shore, where Mrs. Sayther lay down to wait in comfort.

Reclining on her side, she looked out and over the wide-stretching Yukon. Above the mountains which lay beyond the further shore, the sky was murky with the smoke of unseen forest fires, and through this the afternoon sun broke feebly, throwing a vague radiance to earth, and unreal shadows. To the sky-line of the four quarters—spruce-shrouded islands, dark waters, and ice-scarred rocky ridges—stretched the immaculate wilderness. No sign of human existence broke the solitude; no sound the stillness. The land seemed bound under the unreality of the unknown, wrapped in the brooding mystery of great spaces.

Perhaps it was this which made Mrs. Sayther nervous; for

she changed her position constantly, now to look up the river, now down, or to scan the gloomy shores for the half-hidden mouths of back channels. After an hour or so the boatmen were sent ashore to pitch camp for the night, but Pierre remained with his mistress to watch.

"Ah! him come thees tam," he whispered, after a long silence, his gaze bent up the river to the head of the island.

A canoe, with a paddle flashing on either side, was slipping down the current. In the stern a man's form, and in the bow a woman's, swung rhythmically to the work. Mrs. Sayther had no eyes for the woman till the canoe drove in closer and her bizarre beauty peremptorily demanded notice. A close-fitting blouse of moose-skin, fantastically beaded, outlined faithfully the well-rounded lines of her body, while a silken kerchief, gay of color and picturesquely draped, partly covered great masses of blue-black hair. But it was the face, cast belike in copper bronze, which caught and held Mrs. Sayther's fleeting glance. Eyes, piercing and black and large, with a traditionary hint of obliqueness, looked forth from under clear-stencilled, clean-arching brows. Without suggesting cadaverousness, though high-boned and prominent, the cheeks fell away and met in a mouth, thin-lipped and softly strong. It was a face which advertised the dimmest trace of ancient Mongol blood, a reversion, after long centuries of wandering, to the parent stem. This effect was heightened by the delicately aquiline nose with its thin trembling nostrils, and by the general air of eagle wildness which seemed to characterize not only the face but the creature herself. She was, in fact, the Tartar type modified to idealization, and the tribe of Red Indian is lucky that breeds such a unique body once in a score of generations.

Dipping long strokes and strong, the girl, in concert with the man, suddenly whirled the tiny craft about against the current and brought it gently to the shore. Another instant and she stood at the top of the bank, heaving up by rope, hand under hand, a quarter of fresh-killed moose. Then the man followed her, and together, with a swift rush, they drew

23

up the canoe. The dogs were in a whining mass about them, and as the girl stooped among them caressingly, the man's gaze fell upon Mrs. Sayther, who had arisen. He looked, brushed his eyes unconsciously as though his sight were deceiving him, and looked again.

"Karen," he said simply, coming forward and extending his hand, "I thought for the moment I was dreaming. I went snow-blind for a time, this spring, and since then my eyes have been playing tricks with me."

Mrs. Sayther, whose flush had deepened and whose heart was urging painfully, had been prepared for almost anything save this coolly extended hand; but she tactfully curbed herself and grasped it heartily with her own.

"You know, Dave, I threatened often to come, and I would have, too, only—only—"

"Only I didn't give the word." David Payne laughed and watched the Indian girl disappearing into the cabin.

"Oh, I understand, Dave, and had I been in your place I'd most probably have done the same. But I have come—now."

"Then come a little bit farther, into the cabin and get something to eat," he said genially, ignoring or missing the feminine suggestion of appeal in her voice. "And you must be tired too. Which way are you travelling? Up? Then you wintered in Dawson, or came in on the last ice. Your camp?" He glanced at the *voyageurs* circled about the fire in the open, and held back the door for her to enter.

"I came up on the ice from Circle City last winter," he continued, "and settled down here for a while. Am prospecting some on Henderson Creek, and if that fails, have been thinking of trying my hand this fall up the Stuart River."

"You aren't changed much, are you?" she asked irrelevantly,

24

striving to throw the conversation upon a more personal basis.

"A little less flesh, perhaps, and a little more muscle. How did *you* mean?"

But she shrugged her shoulders and peered I through the dim light at the Indian girl, who had lighted the fire and was frying great chunks of moose meat, alternated with thin ribbons of bacon.

"Did you stop in Dawson long?" The man was whittling a stave of birchwood into a rude axe-handle, and asked the question without raising his head.

"Oh, a few days," she answered, following the girl with her eyes, and hardly hearing. "What were you saying? In Dawson? A month, in fact, and glad to get away. The arctic male is elemental, you know, and somewhat strenuous in his feelings."

"Bound to be when he gets right down to the soil. He leaves convention with the spring bed at borne. But you were wise in your choice of time for leaving. You'll be out of the country before mosquito season, which is a blessing your lack of experience will not permit you to appreciate."

"I suppose not. But tell me about yourself, about your life. What kind of neighbors have you? Or have you any?"

While she queried she watched the girl grinding coffee in the corner of a flower sack upon the hearthstone. With a steadiness and skill which predicated nerves as primitive as the method, she crushed the imprisoned berries with a heavy fragment of quartz. David Payne noted his visitor's gaze, and the shadow of a smile drifted over his lips.

"I did have some," he replied. "Missourian chaps, and a couple of Cornishmen, but they went down to Eldorado to work at wages for a grubstake."

25

Mrs. Sayther cast a look of speculative regard upon the girl. "But of course there are plenty of Indians about?"

"Every mother's son of them down to Dawson long ago. Not a native in the whole country, barring Winapie here, and she's a Koyokuk lass,—comes from a thousand miles or so down the river."

Mrs. Sayther felt suddenly faint; and though the smile of interest in no wise waned, the face of the man seemed to draw away to a telescopic distance, and the tiered logs of the cabin to whirl drunkenly about. But she was bidden draw up to the table, and during the meal discovered time and space in which to find herself. She talked little, and that principally about the land and weather, while the man wandered off into a long description of the difference between the shallow summer diggings of the Lower Country and the deep winter diggings of the Upper Country.

"You do not ask why I came north?" she asked. "Surely you know." They had moved back from the table, and David Payne had returned to his axe-handle. "Did you get my letter?"

"A last one? No, I don't think so. Most probably it's trailing around the Birch Creek Country or lying in some trader's shack on the Lower River. The way they run the mails in here is shameful. No order, no system, no—"

"Don't be wooden, Dave! Help me!" She spoke sharply now, with an assumption of authority which rested upon the past. "Why don't you ask me about myself? About those we knew in the old times? Have you no longer any interest in the world? Do you know that my husband is dead?"

"Indeed, I am sorry. How long—"

"David!" She was ready to cry with vexation, but the reproach she threw into her voice eased her.

"Did you get any of my letters? You must have got some of them, though you never answered."

"Well, I didn't get the last one, announcing, evidently, the death of your husband, and most likely others went astray; but I did get some. I—er—read them aloud to Winapie as a warning—that is, you know, to impress upon her the wickedness of her white sisters. And I—er—think she profited by it. Don't you?"

She disregarded the sting, and went on. "In the last letter, which you did not receive, I told, as you have guessed, of Colonel Sayther's death. That was a year ago. I also said that if you did not come out to me, I would go in to you. And as I had often promised, I came."

"I know of no promise."

"In the earlier letters?"

"Yes, you promised, but as I neither asked nor answered, it was unratified. So I do not know of any such promise. But I do know of another, which you, too, may remember. It was very long ago." He dropped the axe-handle to the floor and raised his head. "It was so very long ago, yet I remember it distinctly, the day, the time, every detail. We were in a rose garden, you and I,—your mother's rose garden. All things were budding, blossoming, and the sap of spring was in our blood. And I drew you over—it was the first—and kissed you full on the lips. Don't you remember?"

"Don't go over it, Dave, don't! I know every shameful line of it. How often have I wept! If you only knew how I have suffered—"

"You promised me then—ay, and a thousand times in the sweet days that followed. Each look of your eyes, each touch of your hand, each syllable that fell from your lips, was a promise. And then—how shall I say?—there came a man. He was old—old enough to have begotten you—and not nice

27

to look upon, but as the world goes, clean. He had done no wrong, followed the letter of the law, was respectable. Further, and to the point, he possessed some several paltry mines,—a score; it does not matter: and he owned a few miles of lands, and engineered deals, and clipped coupons. He—"

"But there were other things," she interrupted, "I told you. Pressure—money matters—want—my people—trouble. You understood the whole sordid situation. I could not help it. It was not my will. I was sacrificed, or I sacrificed, have it as you wish. But, my God! Dave, I gave you up! You never did *me* justice. Think what I have gone through!"

"It was not your will? Pressure? Under high heaven there was no thing to will you to this man's bed or that."

"But I cared for you all the time," she pleaded.

"I was unused to your way of measuring love. I am still unused. I do not understand."

"But now! now!"

"We were speaking of this man you saw fit to marry. What manner of man was he? Wherein did he charm your soul? What potent virtues were his? True, he had a golden grip,— an almighty golden grip. He knew the odds. He was versed in cent per cent. He had a narrow wit and excellent judgment of the viler parts, whereby he transferred this man's money to his pockets, and that man's money, and the next man's. And the law smiled. In that it did not condemn, our Christian ethics approved. By social measure he was not a bad man. But by your measure, Karen, by mine, by ours of the rose garden, what was he?"

"Remember, he is dead."

"The fact is not altered thereby. What was he? A great, gross, material creature, deaf to song, blind to beauty, dead

28

to the spirit. He was fat with laziness, and flabby-cheeked, and the round of his belly witnessed his gluttony—"

"But he is dead. It is we who are now—now! now! Don't you hear? As you say, I have been inconstant. I have sinned. Good. But should not you, too, cry *peccavi*? If I have broken promises, have not you? Your love of the rose garden was of all time, or so you said. Where is it now?"

"It is here! now!" he cried, striking his breast passionately with clenched hand. "It has always been."

"And your love was a great love; there was none greater," she continued; "or so you said in the rose garden. Yet it is not fine enough, large enough, to forgive me here, crying now at your feet?"

The man hesitated. His mouth opened; words shaped vainly on his lips. She had forced him to bare his heart and speak truths which he had hidden from himself. And she was good to look upon, standing there in a glory of passion, calling back old associations and warmer life. He turned away his head that he might not see, but she passed around and fronted him.

"Look at me, Dave! Look at me! I am the same, after all. And so are you, if you would but see. We are not changed."

Her hand rested on his shoulder, and his had half-passed, roughly, about her, when the sharp crackle of a match startled him to himself. Winapie, alien to the scene, was lighting the slow wick of the slush lamp. She appeared to start out against a background of utter black, and the flame, flaring suddenly up, lighted her bronze beauty to royal gold.

"You see, it is impossible," he groaned, thrusting the fair-haired woman gently from him. "It is impossible," he repeated. "It is impossible."

"I am not a girl, Dave, with a girl's illusions," she said softly,

29

though not daring to come back to him. "It is as a woman that I understand. Men are men. A common custom of the country. I am not shocked. I divined it from the first. But—ah!—it is only a marriage of the country—not a real marriage?"

"We do not ask such questions in Alaska," he interposed feebly.

"I know, but—"

"Well, then, it is only a marriage of the country—nothing else."

"And there are no children?"

"No."

"Nor—"

"No, no; nothing—but it is impossible."

"But it is not." She was at his side again, her hand touching lightly, caressingly, the sunburned back of his. "I know the custom of the land too well. Men do it every day. They do not care to remain here, shut out from the world, for all their days; so they give an order on the P. C. C. Company for a year's provisions, some money in hand, and the girl is content. By the end of that time, a man—" She shrugged her shoulders. "And so with the girl here. We will give her an order upon the company, not for a year, but for life. What was she when you found her? A raw, meat-eating savage; fish in summer, moose in winter, feasting in plenty, starving in famine. But for you that is what she would have remained. For your coming she was happier; for your going, surely, with a life of comparative splendor assured, she will be happier than if you had never been."

"No, no," he protested. "It is not right."

"Come, Dave, you must see. She is not your kind. There is no race affinity. She is an aborigine, sprung from the soil, yet close to the soil, and impossible to lift from the soil. Born savage, savage she will die. But we—you and I—the dominant, evolved race—the salt of the earth and the masters thereof! We are made for each other. The supreme call is of kind, and we are of kind. Reason and feeling dictate it. Your very instinct demands it. That you cannot deny. You cannot escape the generations behind you. Yours is an ancestry which has survived for a thousand centuries, and for a hundred thousand centuries, and your line must not stop here. It cannot. Your ancestry will not permit it. Instinct is stronger than the will. The race is mightier than you. Come, Dave, let us go. We are young yet, and life is good. Come."

Winapie, passing out of the cabin to feed the dogs, caught his attention and caused him to shake his head and weakly to reiterate. But the woman's hand slipped about his neck, and her cheek pressed to his. His bleak life rose up and smote him,—the vain struggle with pitiless forces; the dreary years of frost and famine; the harsh and jarring contact with elemental life; the aching void which mere animal existence could not fill. And there, seduction by his side, whispering of brighter, warmer lands, of music, light, and joy, called the old times back again. He visioned it unconsciously. Faces rushed in upon him; glimpses of forgotten scenes, memories of merry hours; strains of song and trills of laughter—

"Come, Dave, Come. I have for both. The way is soft." She looked about her at the bare furnishings of the cabin. "I have for both. The world is at our feet, and all joy is ours. Come! come!"

She was in his arms, trembling, and he held her tightly. He rose to his feet . . . But the snarling of hungry dogs, and the shrill cries of Winapie bringing about peace between the combatants, came muffled to his ear through the heavy logs. And another scene flashed before him. A struggle in the forest,—a bald-face grizzly, broken-legged, terrible; the

31

snarling of the dogs and the shrill cries of Winapie as she urged them to the attack; himself in the midst of the crush, breathless, panting, striving to hold off red death; broken-backed, entrail-ripped dogs howling in impotent anguish and desecrating the snow; the virgin white running scarlet with the blood of man and beast; the bear, ferocious, irresistible, crunching, crunching down to the core of his life; and Winapie, at the last, in the thick of the frightful muddle, hair flying, eyes flashing, fury incarnate, passing the long hunting knife again and again—Sweat started to his forehead. He shook off the clinging woman and staggered back to the wall. And she, knowing that the moment had come, but unable to divine what was passing within him, felt all she had gained slipping away.

"Dave! Dave!" she cried. "I will not give you up! I will not give you up! If you do not wish to come, we will stay. I will stay with you. The world is less to me than are you. I will be a Northland wife to you. I will cook your food, feed your dogs, break trail for you, lift a paddle with you. I can do it. Believe me, I am strong."

Nor did he doubt it, looking upon her and holding her off from him; but his face had grown stern and gray, and the warmth had died out of his eyes.

"I will pay off Pierre and the boatmen, and let them go. And I will stay with you, priest or no priest, minister or no minister; go with you, now, anywhere! Dave! Dave! Listen to me! You say I did you wrong in the past—and I did—let me make up for it, let me atone. If I did not rightly measure love before, let me show that I can now."

She sank to the floor and threw her arms about his knees, sobbing. "And you *do* care for me. You *do* care for me. Think! The long years I have waited, suffered! You can never know!" He stooped and raised her to her feet.

"Listen," he commanded, opening the door and lifting her bodily outside. "It cannot be. We are not alone to be

32

considered. You must go. I wish you a safe journey. You will find it tougher work when you get up by the Sixty Mile, but you have the best boatmen in the world, and will get through all right. Will you say good-by?"

Though she already had herself in hand, she looked at him hopelessly. "If—if—if Winapie should—" She quavered and stopped.

But he grasped the unspoken thought, and answered, "Yes." Then struck with the enormity of it, "It cannot be conceived. There is no likelihood. It must not be entertained."

"Kiss me," she whispered, her face lighting. Then she turned and went away.

* * * * *

"Break camp, Pierre," she said to the boatman, who alone had remained awake against her return. "We must be going."

By the firelight his sharp eyes scanned the woe in her face, but he received the extraordinary command as though it were the most usual thing in the world. "*Oui, madame,*" he assented. "Which way? Dawson?"

"No," she answered, lightly enough; "up; out; Dyea."

Whereat he fell upon the sleeping *voyageurs*, kicking them, grunting, from their blankets, and buckling them down to the work, the while his voice, vibrant with action, shrilling through all the camp. In a trice Mrs. Sayther's tiny tent had been struck, pots and pans were being gathered up, blankets rolled, and the men staggering under the loads to the boat. Here, on the banks, Mrs. Sayther waited till the luggage was made ship-shape and her nest prepared.

"We line up to de head of de island," Pierre explained to her while running out the long tow rope. "Den we tak to das

33

back channel, where de water not queek, and I t'ink we mak good tam."

A scuffling and pattering of feet in the last year's dry grass caught his quick ear, and he turned his head. The Indian girl, circled by a bristling ring of wolf dogs, was coming toward them. Mrs. Sayther noted that the girl's face, which had been apathetic throughout the scene in the cabin, had now quickened into blazing and wrathful life.

"What you do my man?" she demanded abruptly of Mrs. Sayther. "Him lay on bunk, and him look bad all the time. I say, 'What the matter, Dave? You sick?' But him no say nothing. After that him say, 'Good girl Winapie, go way. I be all right bimeby.' What you do my man, eh? I think you bad woman."

Mrs. Sayther looked curiously at the barbarian woman who shared the life of this man, while she departed alone in the darkness of night.

"I think you bad woman," Winapie repeated in the slow, methodical way of one who gropes for strange words in an alien tongue. "I think better you go way, no come no more. Eh? What you think? I have one man. I Indian girl. You 'Merican woman. You good to see. You find plenty men. Your eyes blue like the sky. Your skin so white, so soft."

Coolly she thrust out a brown forefinger and pressed the soft cheek of the other woman. And to the eternal credit of Karen Sayther, she never flinched. Pierre hesitated and half stepped forward; but she motioned him away, though her heart welled to him with secret gratitude. "It's all right, Pierre," she said. "Please go away."

He stepped back respectfully out of earshot, where he stood grumbling to himself and measuring the distance in springs.

"Um white, um soft, like baby." Winapie touched the other cheek and withdrew her hand. "Bimeby mosquito come.

Skin get sore in spot; um swell, oh, so big; um hurt, oh, so much. Plenty mosquito; plenty spot. I think better you go now before mosquito come. This way," pointing down the stream, "you go St. Michael's; that way," pointing up, "you go Dyea. Better you go Dyea. Good-by."

And that which Mrs. Sayther then did, caused Pierre to marvel greatly. For she threw her arms around the Indian girl, kissed her, and burst into tears.

"Be good to him," she cried. "Be good to him."

Then she slipped half down the face of the bank, called back "Good-by," and dropped into the boat amidships. Pierre followed her and cast off. He shoved the steering oar into place and gave the signal. Le Goire lifted an old French *chanson*; the men, like a row of ghosts in the dim starlight, bent their backs to the tow line; the steering oar cut the black current sharply, and the boat swept out into the night.

WHICH MAKE MEN REMEMBER

Fortune La Pearle crushed his way through the snow, sobbing, straining, cursing his luck, Alaska, Nome, the cards, and the man who had felt his knife. The hot blood was freezing on his hands, and the scene yet bright in his eyes,—the man, clutching the table and sinking slowly to the floor; the rolling counters and the scattered deck; the swift shiver throughout the room, and the pause; the game-keepers no longer calling, and the clatter of the chips dying away; the startled faces; the infinite instant of silence; and then the great blood-roar and the tide of vengeance which lapped his heels and turned the town mad behind him.

"All hell's broke loose," he sneered, turning aside in the darkness and heading for the beach. Lights were flashing from open doors, and tent, cabin, and dance-hall let slip their denizens upon the chase. The clamor of men and howling of dogs smote his ears and quickened his feet. He ran on and on. The sounds grew dim, and the pursuit dissipated itself in vain rage and aimless groping. But a flitting shadow clung to him. Head thrust over shoulder, he caught glimpses of it, now taking vague shape on an open expanse of snow, how merging into the deeper shadows of some darkened cabin or beach-listed craft.

Fortune La Pearle swore like a woman, weakly, with the hint of tears that comes of exhaustion, and plunged deeper into the maze of heaped ice, tents, and prospect holes. He stumbled over taut hawsers and piles of dunnage, tripped on crazy guy-ropes and insanely planted pegs, and fell again and again upon frozen dumps and mounds of hoarded driftwood. At times, when he deemed he had drawn clear, his head dizzy with the painful pounding of his heart and the suffocating intake of his breath, he slackened down; and ever

36

the shadow leaped out of the gloom and forced him on in heart-breaking flight. A swift intuition lashed upon him, leaving in its trail the cold chill of superstition. The persistence of the shadow he invested with his gambler's symbolism. Silent, inexorable, not to be shaken off, he took it as the fate which waited at the last turn when chips were cashed in and gains and losses counted up. Fortune La Pearle believed in those rare, illuminating moments, when the intelligence flung from it time and space, to rise naked through eternity and read the facts of life from the open book of chance. That this was such a moment he had no doubt; and when he turned inland and sped across the snow-covered tundra he was not startled because the shadow took upon it greater definiteness and drew in closer. Oppressed with his own impotence, he halted in the midst of the white waste and whirled about. His right hand slipped from its mitten, and a revolver, at level, glistened in the pale light of the stars.

"Don't shoot. I haven't a gun."

The shadow had assumed tangible shape, and at the sound of its human voice a trepidation affected Fortune La Pearle's knees, and his stomach was stricken with the qualms of sudden relief.

Perhaps things fell out differently because Uri Bram had no gun that night when he sat on the hard benches of the El Dorado and saw murder done. To that fact also might be attributed the trip on the Long Trail which he took subsequently with a most unlikely comrade. But be it as it may, he repeated a second time, "Don't shoot. Can't you see I haven't a gun?"

"Then what the flaming hell did you take after me for?" demanded the gambler, lowering his revolver.

Uri Bram shrugged his shoulders. "It don't matter much, anyhow. I want you to come with me."

"Where?"

"To my shack, over on the edge of the camp."

But Fortune La Pearle drove the heel of his moccasin into the snow and attested by his various deities to the madness of Uri Bram. "Who are you," he perorated, "and what am I, that I should put my neck into the rope at your bidding?"

"I am Uri Bram," the other said simply, "and my shack is over there on the edge of camp. I don't know who you are, but you've thrust the soul from a living man's body,—there's the blood red on your sleeve,—and, like a second Cain, the hand of all mankind is against you, and there is no place you may lay your head. Now, I have a shack—"

"For the love of your mother, hold your say, man," interrupted Fortune La Pearle, "or I'll make you a second Abel for the joy of it. So help me, I will! With a thousand men to lay me by the heels, looking high and low, what do I want with your shack? I want to get out of here—away! away! away! Cursed swine! I've half a mind to go back and run amuck, and settle for a few of them, the pigs! One gorgeous, glorious fight, and end the whole damn business! It's a skin game, that's what life is, and I'm sick of it!"

He stopped, appalled, crushed by his great desolation, and Uri Bram seized the moment. He was not given to speech, this man, and that which followed was the longest in his life, save one long afterward in another place.

"That's why I told you about my shack. I can stow you there so they'll never find you, and I've got grub in plenty. Elsewise you can't get away. No dogs, no nothing, the sea closed, St. Michael the nearest post, runners to carry the news before you, the same over the portage to Anvik—not a chance in the world for you! Now wait with me till it blows over. They'll forget all about you in a month or less, what of stampeding to York and what not, and you can hit the trail under their noses and they won't bother. I've got my own ideas of justice. When I ran after you, out of the El Dorado and along the beach, it wasn't to catch you or give you up. My ideas are my own, and that's not one of them."

He ceased as the murderer drew a prayer-book from his pocket. With the aurora borealis glimmering yellow in the northeast, heads bared to the frost and naked hands grasping the sacred book, Fortune La Pearle swore him to the words he had spoken—an oath which Uri Bram never intended breaking, and never broke.

At the door of the shack the gambler hesitated for an instant, marvelling at the strangeness of this man who had befriended him, and doubting. But by the candlelight he found the cabin comfortable and without occupants, and he was quickly rolling a cigarette while the other man made coffee. His muscles relaxed in the warmth and he lay back with half-assumed indolence, intently studying Uri's face through the curling wisps of smoke. It was a powerful face, but its strength was of that peculiar sort which stands girt in and unrelated. The seams were deep-graven, more like scars, while the stern features were in no way softened by hints of sympathy or humor. Under prominent bushy brows the eyes shone cold and gray. The cheekbones, high and forbidding, were undermined by deep hollows. The chin and jaw displayed a steadiness of purpose which the narrow forehead advertised as single, and, if needs be, pitiless. Everything was harsh, the nose, the lips, the voice, the lines about the mouth. It was the face of one who communed much with himself, unused to seeking counsel from the world; the face of one who wrestled oft of nights with angels, and rose to face the day with shut lips that no man might know. He was narrow but deep; and Fortune, his own humanity broad and shallow, could make nothing of him. Did Uri sing when merry and sigh when sad, he could have understood; but as it was, the cryptic features were undecipherable; he could not measure the soul they concealed.

"Lend a hand, Mister Man," Uri ordered when the cups had been emptied. "We've got to fix up for visitors."

Fortune purred his name for the other's benefit, and assisted understandingly. The bunk was built against a side and end of the cabin. It was a rude affair, the bottom being composed of drift-wood logs overlaid with moss. At the foot the rough ends of these timbers projected in an uneven row. From the side next the wall Uri ripped back the moss and removed three of the logs. The jagged ends he sawed off and replaced so that the projecting row remained unbroken. Fortune carried in sacks of flour from the cache and piled them on the floor beneath the aperture. On these Uri laid a pair of long sea-bags, and over all spread several thicknesses of moss and blankets. Upon this Fortune could lie, with the sleeping furs stretching over him from one side of the bunk to the other, and all men could look upon it and declare it empty.

In the weeks which followed, several domiciliary visits were paid, not a shack or tent in Nome escaping, but Fortune lay in his cranny undisturbed. In fact, little attention was given to Uri Bram's cabin; for it was the last place under the sun to expect to find the murderer of John Randolph. Except during such interruptions, Fortune lolled about the cabin, playing long games of solitaire and smoking endless cigarettes. Though his volatile nature loved geniality and play of words and laughter, he quickly accommodated himself to Uri's taciturnity. Beyond the actions and plans of his pursuers, the state of the trails, and the price of dogs, they never talked; and these things were only discussed at rare intervals and briefly. But Fortune fell to working out a system, and hour after hour, and day after day, he shuffled and dealt, shuffled and dealt, noted the combinations of the cards in long columns, and shuffled and dealt again. Toward the end even this absorption failed him, and, head bowed upon the table, he visioned the lively all-night houses of Nome, where the gamekeepers and lookouts worked in shifts and the clattering roulette ball never slept. At such times his loneliness and bankruptcy stunned him till he sat for hours in the same unblinking, unchanging position. At other times, his long-pent bitterness found voice in passionate outbursts; for he had rubbed the world the wrong way and did not like the feel of it.

"Life's a skin-game," he was fond of repeating, and on this one note he rang the changes. "I never had half a chance," he complained. "I was faked in my birth and flim-flammed with my mother's milk. The dice were loaded when she tossed the box, and I was born to prove the loss. But that was no reason she should blame me for it, and look on me as a cold deck; but she did—ay, she did. Why didn't she give me a show? Why didn't the world? Why did I go broke in Seattle? Why did I take the steerage, and live like a hog to Nome? Why did I go to the El Dorado? I was heading for Big Pete's and only went for matches. Why didn't I have matches? Why did I want to smoke? Don't you see? All worked out, every bit of it, all parts fitting snug. Before I was born, like as not. I'll put the sack I never hope to get on it, before I was born. That's why! That's why John Randolph passed the word and his checks in at the same time. Damn him! It served him well right! Why didn't he keep his tongue between his teeth and give me a chance? He knew I was next to broke. Why didn't I hold my hand? Oh, why? Why? Why?"

And Fortune La Pearle would roll upon the floor, vainly interrogating the scheme of things. At such outbreaks Uri said no word, gave no sign, save that his grey eyes seemed to turn dull and muddy, as though from lack of interest. There was nothing in common between these two men, and this fact Fortune grasped sufficiently to wonder sometimes why Uri had stood by him.

But the time of waiting came to an end. Even a community's blood lust cannot stand before its gold lust. The murder of John Randolph had already passed into the annals of the camp, and there it rested. Had the murderer appeared, the men of Nome would certainly have stopped stampeding long enough to see justice done, whereas the whereabouts of

41

Fortune La Pearle was no longer an insistent problem. There was gold in the creek beds and ruby beaches, and when the sea opened, the men with healthy sacks would sail away to where the good things of life were sold absurdly cheap.

So, one night, Fortune helped Uri Bram harness the dogs and lash the sled, and the twain took the winter trail south on the ice. But it was not all south; for they left the sea east from St. Michael's, crossed the divide, and struck the Yukon at Anvik, many hundred miles from its mouth. Then on, into the northeast, past Koyokuk, Tanana, and Minook, till they rounded the Great Curve at Fort Yukon, crossed and recrossed the Arctic Circle, and headed south through the Flats. It was a weary journey, and Fortune would have wondered why the man went with him, had not Uri told him that he owned claims and had men working at Eagle. Eagle lay on the edge of the line; a few miles farther on, the British flag waved over the barracks at Fort Cudahy. Then came Dawson, Pelly, the Five Fingers, Windy Arm, Caribou Crossing, Linderman, the Chilcoot and Dyea.

On the morning after passing Eagle, they rose early. This was their last camp, and they were now to part. Fortune's heart was light. There was a promise of spring in the land, and the days were growing longer. The way was passing into Canadian territory. Liberty was at hand, the sun was returning, and each day saw him nearer to the Great Outside. The world was big, and he could once again paint his future in royal red. He whistled about the breakfast and hummed snatches of light song while Uri put the dogs in harness and packed up. But when all was ready, Fortune's feet itching to be off, Uri pulled an unused back-log to the fire and sat down.

"Ever hear of the Dead Horse Trail?"

He glanced up meditatively and Fortune shook his head, inwardly chafing at the delay.

"Sometimes there are meetings under circumstances which

make men remember," Uri continued, speaking in a low voice and very slowly, "and I met a man under such circumstances on the Dead Horse Trail. Freighting an outfit over the White Pass in '97 broke many a man's heart, for there was a world of reason when they gave that trail its name. The horses died like mosquitoes in the first frost, and from Skaguay to Bennett they rotted in heaps. They died at the Rocks, they were poisoned at the Summit, and they starved at the Lakes; they fell off the trail, what there was of it, or they went through it; in the river they drowned under their loads, or were smashed to pieces against the boulders; they snapped their legs in the crevices and broke their backs falling backwards with their packs; in the sloughs they sank from sight or smothered in the slime, and they were disembowelled in the bogs where the corduroy logs turned end up in the mud; men shot them, worked them to death, and when they were gone, went back to the beach and bought more. Some did not bother to shoot them,—stripping the saddles off and the shoes and leaving them where they fell. Their hearts turned to stone—those which did not break—and they became beasts, the men on Dead Horse Trail.

"It was there I met a man with the heart of a Christ and the patience. And he was honest. When he rested at midday he took the packs from the horses so that they, too, might rest. He paid $50 a hundred-weight for their fodder, and more. He used his own bed to blanket their backs when they rubbed raw. Other men let the saddles eat holes the size of water-buckets. Other men, when the shoes gave out, let them wear their hoofs down to the bleeding stumps. He spent his last dollar for horseshoe nails. I know this because we slept in the one bed and ate from the one pot, and became blood brothers where men lost their grip of things and died blaspheming God. He was never too tired to ease a strap or tighten a cinch, and often there were tears in his eyes when he looked on all that waste of misery. At a passage in the rocks, where the brutes upreared hindlegged and stretched their forelegs upward like cats to clear the wall, the way was piled with carcasses where they had toppled back. And here he stood, in the stench of hell, with a cheery word and a hand on the rump at the right time, till the string passed by. And when one bogged he blocked the trail till it was clear again; nor did the man live who crowded him at such time.

"At the end of the trail a man who had killed fifty horses wanted to buy, but we looked at him and at our own,— mountain cayuses from eastern Oregon. Five thousand he offered, and we were broke, but we remembered the poison grass of the Summit and the passage in the Rocks, and the man who was my brother spoke no word, but divided the cayuses into two bunches,—his in the one and mine in the other,—and he looked at me and we understood each other. So he drove mine to the one side and I drove his to the other, and we took with us our rifles and shot them to the last one, while the man who had killed fifty horses cursed us till his throat cracked. But that man, with whom I welded blood-brothership on the Dead Horse Trail—"

"Why, that man was John Randolph," Fortune, sneering the while, completed the climax for him.

Uri nodded, and said, "I am glad you understand."

"I am ready," Fortune answered, the old weary bitterness strong in his face again. "Go ahead, but hurry."

Uri Bram rose to his feet.

"I have had faith in God all the days of my life. I believe He loves justice. I believe He is looking down upon us now, choosing between us. I believe He waits to work His will through my own right arm. And such is my belief, that we will take equal chance and let Him speak His own judgment."

Fortune's heart leaped at the words. He did not know much concerning Uri's God, but he believed in Chance, and Chance had been coming his way ever since the night he ran down

44

the beach and across the snow. "But there is only one gun," he objected.

"We will fire turn about," Uri replied, at the same time throwing out the cylinder of the other man's Colt and examining it.

"And the cards to decide! One hand of seven up!"

Fortune's blood was warming to the game, and he drew the deck from his pocket as Uri nodded. Surely Chance would not desert him now! He thought of the returning sun as he cut for deal, and he thrilled when he found the deal was his. He shuffled and dealt, and Uri cut him the Jack of Spades. They laid down their hands. Uri's was bare of trumps, while he held ace, deuce. The outside seemed very near to him as they stepped off the fifty paces.

"If God withholds His hand and you drop me, the dogs and outfit are yours. You'll find a bill of sale, already made out, in my pocket," Uri explained, facing the path of the bullet, straight and broad-breasted.

Fortune shook a vision of the sun shining on the ocean from his eyes and took aim. He was very careful. Twice he lowered as the spring breeze shook the pines. But the third time he dropped on one knee, gripped the revolver steadily in both hands, and fired. Uri whirled half about, threw up his arms, swayed wildly for a moment, and sank into the snow. But Fortune knew he had fired too far to one side, else the man would not have whirled.

When Uri, mastering the flesh and struggling to his feet, beckoned for the weapon, Fortune was minded to fire again. But he thrust the idea from him. Chance had been very good to him already, he felt, and if he tricked now he would have to pay for it afterward. No, he would play fair. Besides Uri was hard hit and could not possibly hold the heavy Colt long enough to draw a bead.

45

"And where is your God now?" he taunted, as he gave the wounded man the revolver.

And Uri answered: "God has not yet spoken. Prepare that He may speak."

Fortune faced him, but twisted his chest sideways in order to present less surface. Uri tottered about drunkenly, but waited, too, for the moment's calm between the catspaws. The revolver was very heavy, and he doubted, like Fortune, because of its weight. But he held it, arm extended, above his head, and then let it slowly drop forward and down. At the instant Fortune's left breast and the sight flashed into line with his eye, he pulled the trigger. Fortune did not whirl, but gay San Francisco dimmed and faded, and as the sun-bright snow turned black and blacker, he breathed his last malediction on the Chance he had misplayed.

SIWASH

"If I was a man—" Her words were in themselves indecisive, but the withering contempt which flashed from her black eyes was not lost upon the men-folk in the tent.

Tommy, the English sailor, squirmed, but chivalrous old Dick Humphries, Cornish fisherman and erstwhile American salmon capitalist, beamed upon her benevolently as ever. He bore women too large a portion of his rough heart to mind them, as he said, when they were in the doldrums, or when their limited vision would not permit them to see all around a thing. So they said nothing, these two men who had taken the half-frozen woman into their tent three days back, and who had warmed her, and fed her, and rescued her goods from the Indian packers. This latter had necessitated the payment of numerous dollars, to say nothing of a demonstration in force—Dick Humphries squinting along the sights of a Winchester while Tommy apportioned their wages among them at his own appraisement. It had been a little thing in itself, but it meant much to a woman playing a desperate single-hand in the equally desperate Klondike rush of '97. Men were occupied with their own pressing needs, nor did they approve of women playing, single-handed, the odds of the arctic winter. "If I was a man, I know what I would do." Thus reiterated Molly, she of the flashing eyes, and therein spoke the cumulative grit of five American-born generations.

In the succeeding silence, Tommy thrust a pan of biscuits into the Yukon stove and piled on fresh fuel. A reddish flood pounded along under his sun-tanned skin, and as he stooped, the skin of his neck was scarlet. Dick palmed a three-cornered sail needle through a set of broken pack straps, his good nature in nowise disturbed by the feminine

47

cataclysm which was threatening to burst in the storm-beaten tent.

"And if you was a man?" he asked, his voice vibrant with kindness. The three-cornered needle jammed in the damp leather, and he suspended work for the moment.

"I'd be a man. I'd put the straps on my back and light out. I wouldn't lay in camp here, with the Yukon like to freeze most any day, and the goods not half over the portage. And you—you are men, and you sit here, holding your hands, afraid of a little wind and wet. I tell you straight, Yankee-men are made of different stuff. They'd be hitting the trail for Dawson if they had to wade through hell-fire. And you, you—I wish I was a man."

"I'm very glad, my dear, that you're not." Dick Humphries threw the bight of the sail twine over the point of the needle and drew it clear with a couple of deft turns and a jerk.

A snort of the gale dealt the tent a broad-handed slap as it hurtled past, and the sleet rat-tat-tatted with snappy spite against the thin canvas. The smoke, smothered in its exit, drove back through the fire-box door, carrying with it the pungent odor of green spruce.

"Good Gawd! Why can't a woman listen to reason?" Tommy lifted his head from the denser depths and turned upon her a pair of smoke-outraged eyes.

"And why can't a man show his manhood?"

Tommy sprang to his feet with an oath which would have shocked a woman of lesser heart, ripped loose the sturdy reef-knots and flung back the flaps of the tent.

The trio peered out. It was not a heartening spectacle. A few water-soaked tents formed the miserable foreground, from which the streaming ground sloped to a foaming gorge. Down this ramped a mountain torrent. Here and there,

48

dwarf spruce, rooting and grovelling in the shallow alluvium, marked the proximity of the timber line. Beyond, on the opposing slope, the vague outlines of a glacier loomed dead-white through the driving rain. Even as they looked, its massive front crumbled into the valley, on the breast of some subterranean vomit, and it lifted its hoarse thunder above the screeching voice of the storm. Involuntarily, Molly shrank back.

"Look, woman! Look with all your eyes! Three miles in the teeth of the gale to Crater Lake, across two glaciers, along the slippery rim-rock, knee-deep in a howling river! Look, I say, you Yankee woman! Look! There's your Yankee-men!" Tommy pointed a passionate hand in the direction of the struggling tents. "Yankees, the last mother's son of them. Are they on trail? Is there one of them with the straps to his back? And you would teach us men our work? Look, I say!"

Another tremendous section of the glacier rumbled earthward. The wind whipped in at the open doorway, bulging out the sides of the tent till it swayed like a huge bladder at its guy ropes. The smoke swirled about them, and the sleet drove sharply into their flesh. Tommy pulled the flaps together hastily, and returned to his tearful task at the fire-box. Dick Humphries threw the mended pack straps into a corner and lighted his pipe. Even Molly was for the moment persuaded.

"There's my clothes," she half-whimpered, the feminine for the moment prevailing. "They're right at the top of the cache, and they'll be ruined! I tell you, ruined!"

"There, there," Dick interposed, when the last quavering syllable had wailed itself out. "Don't let that worry you, little woman. I'm old enough to be your father's brother, and I've a daughter older than you, and I'll tog you out in fripperies when we get to Dawson if it takes my last dollar."

"When we get to Dawson!" The scorn had come back to her

49

throat with a sudden surge. "You'll rot on the way, first. You'll drown in a mudhole. You—you—Britishers!"

The last word, explosive, intensive, had strained the limits of her vituperation. If that would not stir these men, what could? Tommy's neck ran red again, but he kept his tongue between his teeth. Dick's eyes mellowed. He had the advantage over Tommy, for he had once had a white woman for a wife.

The blood of five American-born generations is, under certain circumstances, an uncomfortable heritage; and among these circumstances might be enumerated that of being quartered with next of kin. These men were Britons. On sea and land her ancestry and the generations thereof had thrashed them and theirs. On sea and land they would continue to do so. The traditions of her race clamored for vindication. She was but a woman of the present, but in her bubbled the whole mighty past. It was not alone Molly Travis who pulled on gum boots, mackintosh, and straps; for the phantom hands of ten thousand forbears drew tight the buckles, just so as they squared her jaw and set her eyes with determination. She, Molly Travis, intended to shame these Britishers; they, the innumerable shades, were asserting the dominance of the common race.

The men-folk did not interfere. Once Dick suggested that she take his oilskins, as her mackintosh was worth no more than paper in such a storm. But she sniffed her independence so sharply that he communed with his pipe till she tied the flaps on the outside and slushed away on the flooded trail.

"Think she'll make it?" Dick's face belied the indifference of his voice.

"Make it? If she stands the pressure till she gets to the cache, what of the cold and misery, she'll be stark, raving mad. Stand it? She'll be dumb-crazed. You know it yourself, Dick. You've wind-jammed round the Horn. You

50

know what it is to lay out on a topsail yard in the thick of it, bucking sleet and snow and frozen canvas till you're ready to just let go and cry like a baby. Clothes? She won't be able to tell a bundle of skirts from a gold pan or a tea-kettle."

"Kind of think we were wrong in letting her go, then?"

"Not a bit of it. So help me, Dick, she'd 'a' made this tent a hell for the rest of the trip if we hadn't. Trouble with her she's got too much spirit. This'll tone it down a bit."

"Yes," Dick admitted, "she's too ambitious. But then Molly's all right. A cussed little fool to tackle a trip like this, but a plucky sight better than those pick-me-up-and-carry-me kind of women. She's the stock that carried you and me, Tommy, and you've got to make allowance for the spirit. Takes a woman to breed a man. You can't suck manhood from the dugs of a creature whose only claim to womanhood is her petticoats. Takes a she-cat, not a cow, to mother a tiger."

"And when they're unreasonable we've got to put up with it, eh?"

"The proposition. A sharp sheath-knife cuts deeper on a slip than a dull one; but that's no reason for to hack the edge off over a capstan bar."

"All right, if you say so, but when it comes to woman, I guess I'll take mine with a little less edge."

"What do you know about it?" Dick demanded.

"Some." Tommy reached over for a pair of Molly's wet stockings and stretched them across his knees to dry.

Dick, eying him querulously, went fishing in her hand satchel, then hitched up to the front of the stove with divers articles of damp clothing spread likewise to the heat.

"Thought you said you never were married?" he asked.

"Did I? No more was I—that is—yes, by Gawd! I was. And as good a woman as ever cooked grub for a man."

"Slipped her moorings?" Dick symbolized infinity with a wave of his hand.

"Ay."

"Childbirth," he added, after a moment's pause.

The beans bubbled rowdily on the front lid, and he pushed the pot back to a cooler surface. After that he investigated the biscuits, tested them with a splinter of wood, and placed them aside under cover of a damp cloth. Dick, after the manner of his kind, stifled his interest and waited silently. "A different woman to Molly. Siwash."

Dick nodded his understanding.

"Not so proud and wilful, but stick by a fellow through thick and thin. Sling a paddle with the next and starve as contentedly as Job. Go for'ard when the sloop's nose was more often under than not, and take in sail like a man. Went prospecting once, up Teslin way, past Surprise Lake and the Little Yellow-Head. Grub gave out, and we ate the dogs. Dogs gave out, and we ate harnesses, moccasins, and furs. Never a whimper; never a pick-me-up-and-carry-me. Before we went she said look out for grub, but when it happened, never a I-told-you-so. 'Never mind, Tommy,' she'd say, day after day, that weak she could bare lift a snow-shoe and her feet raw with the work. 'Never mind. I'd sooner be flat-bellied of hunger and be your woman, Tommy, than have a *potlach* every day and be Chief George's *klooch*.' George was chief of the Chilcoots, you know, and wanted her bad.

"Great days, those. Was a likely chap myself when I struck the coast. Jumped a whaler, the *Pole Star*, at Unalaska, and worked my way down to Sitka on an otter hunter. Picked up with Happy Jack there—know him?"

"Had charge of my traps for me," Dick answered, "down on the Columbia. Pretty wild, wasn't he, with a warm place in his heart for whiskey and women?"

"The very chap. Went trading with him for a couple of seasons—*hooch*, and blankets, and such stuff. Then got a sloop of my own, and not to cut him out, came down Juneau way. That's where I met Killisnoo; I called her Tilly for short. Met her at a squaw dance down on the beach. Chief George had finished the year's trade with the Sticks over the Passes, and was down from Dyea with half his tribe. No end of Siwashes at the dance, and I the only white. No one knew me, barring a few of the bucks I'd met over Sitka way, but I'd got most of their histories from Happy Jack.

"Everybody talking Chinook, not guessing that I could spit it better than most; and principally two girls who'd run away from Haine's Mission up the Lynn Canal. They were trim creatures, good to the eye, and I kind of thought of casting that way; but they were fresh as fresh-caught cod. Too much edge, you see. Being a new-comer, they started to twist me, not knowing I gathered in every word of Chinook they uttered.

"I never let on, but set to dancing with Tilly, and the more we danced the more our hearts warmed to each other. 'Looking for a woman,' one of the girls says, and the other tosses her head and answers, 'Small chance he'll get one when the women are looking for men.' And the bucks and squaws standing around began to grin and giggle and repeat what had been said. 'Quite a pretty boy,' says the first one. I'll not deny I was rather smooth-faced and youngish, but I'd been a man amongst men many's the day, and it rankled me. 'Dancing with Chief George's girl,' pipes the second. 'First thing George'll give him the flat of a paddle and send him about his business.' Chief George had been looking pretty black up to now, but at this he laughed and slapped his knees. He was a husky beggar and would have used the paddle too.

"'Who's the girls?' I asked Tilly, as we went ripping down the centre in a reel. And as soon as she told me their names I remembered all about them from Happy Jack. Had their pedigree down fine—several things he'd told me that not even their own tribe knew. But I held my hush, and went on courting Tilly, they a-casting sharp remarks and everybody roaring. 'Bide a wee, Tommy,' I says to myself; 'bide a wee.'

"And bide I did, till the dance was ripe to break up, and Chief George had brought a paddle all ready for me. Everybody was on the lookout for mischief when we stopped; but I marched, easy as you please, slap into the thick of them. The Mission girls cut me up something clever, and for all I was angry I had to set my teeth to keep from laughing. I turned upon them suddenly.

"'Are you done?' I asked.

"You should have seen them when they heard me spitting Chinook. Then I broke loose. I told them all about themselves, and their people before them; their fathers, mothers, sisters, brothers—everybody, everything. Each mean trick they'd played; every scrape they'd got into; every shame that'd fallen them. And I burned them without fear or favor. All hands crowded round. Never had they heard a white man sling their lingo as I did. Everybody was laughing save the Mission girls. Even Chief George forgot the paddle, or at least he was swallowing too much respect to dare to use it.

"But the girls. 'Oh, don't, Tommy,' they cried, the tears running down their cheeks. 'Please don't. We'll be good. Sure, Tommy, sure.' But I knew them well, and I scorched them on every tender spot. Nor did I slack away till they came down on their knees, begging and pleading with me to keep quiet. Then I shot a glance at Chief George; but he did not know whether to have at me or not, and passed it off by laughing hollowly.

"So be. When I passed the parting with Tilly that night I gave her the word that I was going to be around for a week or so, and that I wanted to see more of her. Not thick-skinned, her kind, when it came to showing like and dislike, and she looked her pleasure for the honest girl she was. Ay, a striking lass, and I didn't wonder that Chief George was taken with her.

"Everything my way. Took the wind from his sails on the first leg. I was for getting her aboard and sailing down Wrangel way till it blew over, leaving him to whistle; but I wasn't to get her that easy. Seems she was living with an uncle of hers—guardian, the way such things go—and seems he was nigh to shuffling off with consumption or some sort of lung trouble. He was good and bad by turns, and she wouldn't leave him till it was over with. Went up to the tepee just before I left, to speculate on how long it'd be; but the old beggar had promised her to Chief George, and when he clapped eyes on me his anger brought on a hemorrhage.

"'Come and take me, Tommy,' she says when we bid good-by on the beach. 'Ay,' I answers; 'when you give the word.' And I kissed her, white-man-fashion and lover-fashion, till she was all of a tremble like a quaking aspen, and I was so beside myself I'd half a mind to go up and give the uncle a lift over the divide.

"So I went down Wrangel way, past St. Mary's and even to the Queen Charlottes, trading, running whiskey, turning the sloop to most anything. Winter was on, stiff and crisp, and I was back to Juneau, when the word came. 'Come,' the beggar says who brought the news. 'Killisnoo say, "Come now."' 'What's the row?' I asks. 'Chief George,' says he. '*Potlach*. Killisnoo, makum *klooch*.'

"Ay, it was bitter—the Taku howling down out of the north, the salt water freezing quick as it struck the deck, and the old sloop and I hammering into the teeth of it for a hundred miles to Dyea. Had a Douglass Islander for crew when I started, but midway up he was washed over from the bows. Jibed all over and crossed the course three times, but never a sign of him."

"Doubled up with the cold most likely," Dick suggested, putting a pause into the narrative while he hung one of Molly's skirts up to dry, "and went down like a pot of lead."

"My idea. So I finished the course alone, half-dead when I made Dyea in the dark of the evening. The tide favored, and I ran the sloop plump to the bank, in the shelter of the river. Couldn't go an inch further, for the fresh water was frozen solid. Halyards and blocks were that iced up I didn't dare lower mainsail or jib. First I broached a pint of the cargo raw, and then, leaving all standing, ready for the start, and with a blanket around me, headed across the flat to the camp. No mistaking, it was a grand layout. The Chilcats had come in a body—dogs, babies, and canoes—to say nothing of the Dog-Ears, the Little Salmons, and the Missions. Full half a thousand of them to celebrate Tilly's wedding, and never a white man in a score of miles.

"Nobody took note of me, the blanket over my head and hiding my face, and I waded knee deep through the dogs and youngsters till I was well up to the front. The show was being pulled off in a big open place among the trees, with great fires burning and the snow moccasin-packed as hard as Portland cement. Next me was Tilly, beaded and scarlet-clothed galore, and against her Chief George and his head men. The shaman was being helped out by the big medicines from the other tribes, and it shivered my spine up and down, the deviltries they cut. I caught myself wondering if the folks in Liverpool could only see me now; and I thought of yellow-haired Gussie, whose brother I licked after my first voyage, just because he was not for having a sailorman courting his sister. And with Gussie in my eyes I looked at Tilly. A rum old world, thinks I, with man a-stepping in trails the mother little dreamed of when he lay at suck.

56

"So be. When the noise was loudest, walrus hides booming and priests a-singing, I says, 'Are you ready?' Gawd! Not a start, not a shot of the eyes my way, not the twitch of a muscle. 'I knew,' she answers, slow and steady as a calm spring tide. 'Where?' 'The high bank at the edge of the ice,' I whispers back. 'Jump out when I give the word.'

"Did I say there was no end of huskies? Well, there was no end. Here, there, everywhere, they were scattered about,— tame wolves and nothing less. When the strain runs thin they breed them in the bush with the wild, and they're bitter fighters. Right at the toe of my moccasin lay a big brute, and by the heel another. I doubled the first one's tail, quick, till it snapped in my grip. As his jaws clipped together where my hand should have been, I threw the second one by the scruff straight into his mouth. 'Go!' I cried to Tilly.

"You know how they fight. In the wink of an eye there was a raging hundred of them, top and bottom, ripping and tearing each other, kids and squaws tumbling which way, and the camp gone wild. Tilly'd slipped away, so I followed. But when I looked over my shoulder at the skirt of the crowd, the devil laid me by the heart, and I dropped the blanket and went back.

"By then the dogs'd been knocked apart and the crowd was untangling itself. Nobody was in proper place, so they didn't note that Tilly'd gone. 'Hello,' I says, gripping Chief George by the hand. 'May your potlach-smoke rise often, and the Sticks bring many furs with the spring.'

"Lord love me, Dick, but he was joyed to see me,—him with the upper hand and wedding Tilly. Chance to puff big over me. The tale that I was hot after her had spread through the camps, and my presence did him proud. All hands knew me, without my blanket, and set to grinning and giggling. It was rich, but I made it richer by playing unbeknowing.

"'What's the row?' I asks. 'Who's getting married now?'

"'Chief George,' the shaman says, ducking his reverence to him.

"'Thought he had two *klooches*.'

"'Him takum more,—three,' with another duck.

"'Oh!' And I turned away as though it didn't interest me.

"But this wouldn't do, and everybody begins singing out, 'Killisnoo! Killisnoo!'

"'Killisnoo what?' I asked.

"'Killisnoo, *klooch*, Chief George,' they blathered. 'Killisnoo, *klooch*.'

"I jumped and looked at Chief George. He nodded his head and threw out his chest.

"'She'll be no *klooch* of yours,' I says solemnly. 'No *klooch* of yours,' I repeats, while his face went black and his hand began dropping to his hunting-knife.

"'Look!' I cries, striking an attitude. 'Big Medicine. You watch my smoke.'

"I pulled off my mittens, rolled back my sleeves, and made half-a-dozen passes in the air.

"'Killisnoo!' I shouts. 'Killisnoo! Killisnoo!'

"I was making medicine, and they began to scare. Every eye was on me; no time to find out that Tilly wasn't there. Then I called Killisnoo three times again, and waited; and three times more. All for mystery and to make them nervous. Chief George couldn't guess what I was up to, and wanted to put a stop to the foolery; but the shamans said to wait, and that they'd see me and go me one better, or words to that effect. Besides, he was a superstitious cuss, and I fancy a bit afraid of the white man's magic.

"Then I called Killisnoo, long and soft like the howl of a wolf, till the women were all a-tremble and the bucks looking serious.

"'Look!' I sprang for'ard, pointing my finger into a bunch of squaws—easier to deceive women than men, you know. 'Look!' And I raised it aloft as though following the flight of a bird. Up, up, straight overhead, making to follow it with my eyes till it disappeared in the sky.

"'Killisnoo,' I said, looking at Chief George and pointing upward again. 'Killisnoo.'

"So help me, Dick, the gammon worked. Half of them, at least, saw Tilly disappear in the air. They'd drunk my whiskey at Juneau and seen stranger sights, I'll warrant. Why should I not do this thing, I, who sold bad spirits corked in bottles? Some of the women shrieked. Everybody fell to whispering in bunches. I folded my arms and held my head high, and they drew further away from me. The time was ripe to go. 'Grab him,' Chief George cries. Three or four of them came at me, but I whirled, quick, made a couple of passes like to send them after Tilly, and pointed up. Touch me? Not for the kingdoms of the earth. Chief George harangued them, but he couldn't get them to lift a leg. Then he made to take me himself; but I repeated the mummery and his grit went out through his fingers.

"'Let your shamans work wonders the like of which I have done this night,' I says. 'Let them call Killisnoo down out of the sky whither I have sent her.' But the priests knew their limits. 'May your *klooches* bear you sons as the spawn of the salmon,' I says, turning to go; 'and may your totem pole stand long in the land, and the smoke of your camp rise always.'

"But if the beggars could have seen me hitting the high

places for the sloop as soon as I was clear of them, they'd thought my own medicine had got after me. Tilly'd kept warm by chopping the ice away, and was all ready to cast off. Gawd! how we ran before it, the Taku howling after us and the freezing seas sweeping over at every clip. With everything battened down, me a-steering and Tilly chopping ice, we held on half the night, till I plumped the sloop ashore on Porcupine Island, and we shivered it out on the beach; blankets wet, and Tilly drying the matches on her breast.

"So I think I know something about it. Seven years, Dick, man and wife, in rough sailing and smooth. And then she died, in the heart of the winter, died in childbirth, up there on the Chilcat Station. She held my hand to the last, the ice creeping up inside the door and spreading thick on the gut of the window. Outside, the lone howl of the wolf and the Silence; inside, death and the Silence. You've never heard the Silence yet, Dick, and Gawd grant you don't ever have to hear it when you sit by the side of death. Hear it? Ay, till the breath whistles like a siren, and the heart booms, booms, booms, like the surf on the shore.

"Siwash, Dick, but a woman. White, Dick, white, clear through. Towards the last she says, 'Keep my feather bed, Tommy, keep it always.' And I agreed. Then she opened her eyes, full with the pain. 'I've been a good woman to you, Tommy, and because of that I want you to promise—to promise'—the words seemed to stick in her throat—'that when you marry, the woman be white. No more Siwash, Tommy. I know. Plenty white women down to Juneau now. I know. Your people call you "squaw-man," your women turn their heads to the one side on the street, and you do not go to their cabins like other men. Why? Your wife Siwash. Is it not so? And this is not good. Wherefore I die. Promise me. Kiss me in token of your promise.'

"I kissed her, and she dozed off, whispering, 'It is good.' At the end, that near gone my ear was at her lips, she roused for the last time. 'Remember, Tommy; remember my feather

60

bed.' Then she died, in childbirth, up there on the Chilcat Station."

The tent heeled over and half flattened before the gale. Dick refilled his pipe, while Tommy drew the tea and set it aside against Molly's return.

And she of the flashing eyes and Yankee blood? Blinded, falling, crawling on hand and knee, the wind thrust back in her throat by the wind, she was heading for the tent. On her shoulders a bulky pack caught the full fury of the storm. She plucked feebly at the knotted flaps, but it was Tommy and Dick who cast them loose. Then she set her soul for the last effort, staggered in, and fell exhausted on the floor.

Tommy unbuckled the straps and took the pack from her. As he lifted it there was a clanging of pots and pans. Dick, pouring out a mug of whiskey, paused long enough to pass the wink across her body. Tommy winked back. His lips pursed the monosyllable, "clothes," but Dick shook his head reprovingly. "Here, little woman," he said, after she had drunk the whiskey and straightened up a bit.

"Here's some dry togs. Climb into them. We're going out to extra-peg the tent. After that, give us the call, and we'll come in and have dinner. Sing out when you're ready."

"So help me, Dick, that's knocked the edge off her for the rest of this trip," Tommy spluttered as they crouched to the lee of the tent.

"But it's the edge is her saving grace." Dick replied, ducking his head to a volley of sleet that drove around a corner of the canvas. "The edge that you and I've got, Tommy, and the edge of our mothers before us."

THE MAN WITH THE GASH

Jacob Kent had suffered from cupidity all the days of his life. This, in turn, had engendered a chronic distrustfulness, and his mind and character had become so warped that he was a very disagreeable man to deal with. He was also a victim to somnambulic propensities, and very set in his ideas. He had been a weaver of cloth from the cradle, until the fever of Klondike had entered his blood and torn him away from his loom. His cabin stood midway between Sixty Mile Post and the Stuart River; and men who made it a custom to travel the trail to Dawson, likened him to a robber baron, perched in his fortress and exacting toll from the caravans that used his ill-kept roads. Since a certain amount of history was required in the construction of this figure, the less cultured wayfarers from Stuart River were prone to describe him after a still more primordial fashion, in which a command of strong adjectives was to be chiefly noted.

This cabin was not his, by the way, having been built several years previously by a couple of miners who had got out a raft of logs at that point for a grub-stake. They had been most hospitable lads, and, after they abandoned it, travelers who knew the route made it an object to arrive there at nightfall. It was very handy, saving them all the time and toil of pitching camp; and it was an unwritten rule that the last man left a neat pile of firewood for the next comer. Rarely a night passed but from half a dozen to a score of men crowded into its shelter. Jacob Kent noted these things, exercised squatter sovereignty, and moved in. Thenceforth, the weary travelers were mulcted a dollar per head for the privilege of sleeping on the floor, Jacob Kent weighing the dust and never failing to steal the down-weight. Besides, he so contrived that his transient guests chopped his wood for him and carried his water. This was rank piracy, but his victims were an easy-going breed, and while they detested him, they yet permitted him to flourish in his sins.

One afternoon in April he sat by his door,—for all the world like a predatory spider,—marvelling at the heat of the returning sun, and keeping an eye on the trail for prospective flies. The Yukon lay at his feet, a sea of ice, disappearing around two great bends to the north and south, and stretching an honest two miles from bank to bank. Over its rough breast ran the sled-trail, a slender sunken line, eighteen inches wide and two thousand miles in length, with more curses distributed to the linear foot than any other road in or out of all Christendom.

Jacob Kent was feeling particularly good that afternoon. The record had been broken the previous night, and he had sold his hospitality to no less than twenty-eight visitors. True, it had been quite uncomfortable, and four had snored beneath his bunk all night; but then it had added appreciable weight to the sack in which he kept his gold dust. That sack, with its glittering yellow treasure, was at once the chief delight and the chief bane of his existence. Heaven and hell lay within its slender mouth. In the nature of things, there being no privacy to his one-roomed dwelling, he was tortured by a constant fear of theft. It would be very easy for these bearded, desperate-looking strangers to make away with it. Often he dreamed that such was the case, and awoke in the grip of nightmare. A select number of these robbers haunted him through his dreams, and he came to know them quite well, especially the bronzed leader with the gash on his right cheek. This fellow was the most persistent of the lot, and, because of him, he had, in his waking moments, constructed several score of hiding-places in and about the cabin. After a concealment he would breathe freely again, perhaps for several nights, only to collar the Man with the Gash in the very act of unearthing the sack. Then, on awakening in the midst of the usual struggle, he would at once get up and transfer the bag to a new and more ingenious crypt. It was not that he was the direct victim of these phantasms; but he believed in omens and thought-transference, and he deemed these dream-robbers to be the astral projection of real personages who happened at those particular moments, no matter where they were in the flesh, to be harboring designs, in the spirit, upon his wealth. So he continued to bleed the unfortunates who crossed his threshold, and at the same time to add to his trouble with every ounce that went into the sack.

As he sat sunning himself, a thought came to Jacob Kent that brought him to his feet with a jerk. The pleasures of life had culminated in the continual weighing and reweighing of his dust; but a shadow had been thrown upon this pleasant avocation, which he had hitherto failed to brush aside. His gold-scales were quite small; in fact, their maximum was a pound and a half,—eighteen ounces,—while his hoard mounted up to something like three and a third times that. He had never been able to weigh it all at one operation, and hence considered himself to have been shut out from a new and most edifying coign of contemplation. Being denied this, half the pleasure of possession had been lost; nay, he felt that this miserable obstacle actually minimized the fact, as it did the strength, of possession. It was the solution of this problem flashing across his mind that had just brought him to his feet. He searched the trail carefully in either direction. There was nothing in sight, so he went inside.

In a few seconds he had the table cleared away and the scales set up. On one side he placed the stamped disks to the equivalent of fifteen ounces, and balanced it with dust on the other. Replacing the weights with dust, he then had thirty ounces precisely balanced. These, in turn, he placed together on one side and again balanced with more dust. By this time the gold was exhausted, and he was sweating liberally. He trembled with ecstasy, ravished beyond measure. Nevertheless he dusted the sack thoroughly, to the last least grain, till the balance was overcome and one side of the scales sank to the table. Equilibrium, however, was restored by the addition of a pennyweight and five grains to the opposite side. He stood, head thrown back, transfixed.

The sack was empty, but the potentiality of the scales had become immeasurable. Upon them he could weigh any amount, from the tiniest grain to pounds upon pounds. Mammon laid hot fingers on his heart. The sun swung on its westering way till it flashed through the open doorway, full upon the yellow-burdened scales. The precious heaps, like the golden breasts of a bronze Cleopatra, flung back the light in a mellow glow. Time and space were not.

"Gawd blime me! but you 'ave the makin' of several quid there, 'aven't you?"

Jacob Kent wheeled about, at the same time reaching for his double-barrelled shotgun, which stood handy. But when his eyes lit on the intruder's face, he staggered back dizzily. *It was the face of the Man with the Gash!*

The man looked at him curiously.

"Oh, that's all right," he said, waving his hand deprecatingly. "You needn't think as I'll 'arm you or your blasted dust.

"You're a rum 'un, you are," he added reflectively, as he watched the sweat pouring from off Kent's face and the quavering of his knees.

"W'y don't you pipe up an' say somethin'?" he went on, as the other struggled for breath. "Wot's gone wrong o' your gaff? Anythink the matter?"

"W—w—where'd you get it?" Kent at last managed to articulate, raising a shaking forefinger to the ghastly scar which seamed the other's cheek.

"Shipmate stove me down with a marlin-spike from the main-royal. An' now as you 'ave your figger'ead in trim, wot I want to know is, wot's it to you? That's wot I want to know— wot's it to you? Gawd blime me! do it 'urt you? Ain't it smug enough for the likes o' you? That's wot I want to know!"

65

"No, no," Kent answered, sinking upon a stool with a sickly grin. "I was just wondering."

"Did you ever see the like?" the other went on truculently.

"No."

"Ain't it a beute?"

"Yes." Kent nodded his head approvingly, intent on humoring this strange visitor, but wholly unprepared for the outburst which was to follow his effort to be agreeable.

"You blasted, bloomin', burgoo-eatin' son-of-a-sea-swab! Wot do you mean, a sayin' the most onsightly thing Gawd Almighty ever put on the face o' man is a beute? Wot do you mean, you—"

And thereat this fiery son of the sea broke off into a string of Oriental profanity, mingling gods and devils, lineages and men, metaphors and monsters, with so savage a virility that Jacob Kent was paralyzed. He shrank back, his arms lifted as though to ward off physical violence. So utterly unnerved was he that the other paused in the mid-swing of a gorgeous peroration and burst into thunderous laughter.

"The sun's knocked the bottom out o' the trail," said the Man with the Gash, between departing paroxysms of mirth. "An' I only 'ope as you'll appreciate the hoppertunity of consortin' with a man o' my mug. Get steam up in that fire-box o' your'n. I'm goin' to unrig the dogs an' grub 'em. An' don't be shy o' the wood, my lad; there's plenty more where that come from, and it's you've got the time to sling an axe. An' tote up a bucket o' water while you're about it. Lively! or I'll run you down, so 'elp me!"

Such a thing was unheard of. Jacob Kent was making the fire, chopping wood, packing water—doing menial tasks for a guest! When Jim Cardegee left Dawson, it was with his head filled with the iniquities of this roadside Shylock; and all along the trail his numerous victims had added to the sum of his crimes. Now, Jim Cardegee, with the sailor's love for a sailor's joke, had determined, when he pulled into the cabin, to bring its inmate down a peg or so. That he had succeeded beyond expectation he could not help but remark, though he was in the dark as to the part the gash on his cheek had played in it. But while he could not understand, he saw the terror it created, and resolved to exploit it as remorselessly as would any modern trader a choice bit of merchandise.

"Strike me blind, but you're a 'ustler," he said admiringly, his head cocked to one side, as his host bustled about. "You never 'ort to 'ave gone Klondiking. It's the keeper of a pub' you was laid out for. An' it's often as I 'ave 'eard the lads up an' down the river speak o' you, but I 'adn't no idea you was so jolly nice."

Jacob Kent experienced a tremendous yearning to try his shotgun on him, but the fascination of the gash was too potent. This was the real Man with the Gash, the man who had so often robbed him in the spirit. This, then, was the embodied entity of the being whose astral form had been projected into his dreams, the man who had so frequently harbored designs against his hoard; hence—there could be no other conclusion—this Man with the Gash had now come in the flesh to dispossess him. And that gash! He could no more keep his eyes from it than stop the beating of his heart. Try as he would, they wandered back to that one point as inevitably as the needle to the pole.

"Do it 'urt you?" Jim Cardegee thundered suddenly, looking up from the spreading of his blankets and encountering the rapt gaze of the other. "It strikes me as 'ow it 'ud be the proper thing for you to draw your jib, douse the glim, an' turn in, seein' as 'ow it worrits you. Jes' lay to that, you swab, or so 'elp me I'll take a pull on your peak-purchases!"

Kent was so nervous that it took three puffs to blow out the slush-lamp, and he crawled into his blankets without even removing his moccasins. The sailor was soon snoring lustily from his hard bed on the floor, but Kent lay staring up into the blackness, one hand on the shotgun, resolved not to close his eyes the whole night. He had not had an opportunity to secrete his five pounds of gold, and it lay in the ammunition box at the head of his bunk. But, try as he would, he at last dozed off with the weight of his dust heavy on his soul. Had he not inadvertently fallen asleep with his mind in such condition, the somnambulic demon would not have been invoked, nor would Jim Cardegee have gone mining next day with a dish-pan.

The fire fought a losing battle, and at last died away, while the frost penetrated the mossy chinks between the logs and chilled the inner atmosphere. The dogs outside ceased their howling, and, curled up in the snow, dreamed of salmon-stocked heavens where dog-drivers and kindred task-masters were not. Within, the sailor lay like a log, while his host tossed restlessly about, the victim of strange fantasies. As midnight drew near he suddenly threw off the blankets and got up. It was remarkable that he could do what he then did without ever striking a light. Perhaps it was because of the darkness that he kept his eyes shut, and perhaps it was for fear he would see the terrible gash on the cheek of his visitor; but, be this as it may, it is a fact that, unseeing, he opened his ammunition box, put a heavy charge into the muzzle of the shotgun without spilling a particle, rammed it down with double wads, and then put everything away and got back into bed.

Just as daylight laid its steel-gray fingers on the parchment window, Jacob Kent awoke. Turning on his elbow, he raised the lid and peered into the ammunition box. Whatever he saw, or whatever he did not see, exercised a very peculiar effect upon him, considering his neurotic temperament. He glanced at the sleeping man on the floor, let the lid down gently, and rolled over on his back. It was an unwonted calm that rested on his face. Not a muscle quivered. There was not the least sign of excitement or perturbation. He lay there a long while, thinking, and when he got up and began to move about, it was in a cool, collected manner, without noise and without hurry.

It happened that a heavy wooden peg had been driven into the ridge-pole just above Jim Cardegee's head. Jacob Kent, working softly, ran a piece of half-inch manila over it, bringing both ends to the ground. One end he tied about his waist, and in the other he rove a running noose. Then he cocked his shotgun and laid it within reach, by the side of numerous moose-hide thongs. By an effort of will he bore the sight of the scar, slipped the noose over the sleeper's head, and drew it taut by throwing back on his weight, at the same time seizing the gun and bringing it to bear.

Jim Cardegee awoke, choking, bewildered, staring down the twin wells of steel.

"Where is it?" Kent asked, at the same time slacking on the rope.

"You blasted—ugh—"

Kent merely threw back his weight, shutting off the other's wind.

"Bloomin'—Bur—ugh—"

"Where is it?" Kent repeated.

"Wot?" Cardegee asked, as soon as he had caught his breath.

"The gold-dust."

"Wot gold-dust?" the perplexed sailor demanded.

"You know well enough,—mine."

"Ain't seen nothink of it. Wot do ye take me for? A safe-deposit? Wot 'ave I got to do with it, any'ow?"

"Mebbe you know, and mebbe you don't know, but anyway, I'm going to stop your breath till you do know. And if you lift a hand, I'll blow your head off!"

"Vast heavin'!" Cardegee roared, as the rope tightened.

Kent eased away a moment, and the sailor, wriggling his neck as though from the pressure, managed to loosen the noose a bit and work it up so the point of contact was just under the chin.

"Well?" Kent questioned, expecting the disclosure.

But Cardegee grinned. "Go ahead with your 'angin', you bloomin' old pot-wolloper!"

Then, as the sailor had anticipated, the tragedy became a farce. Cardegee being the heavier of the two, Kent, throwing his body backward and down, could not lift him clear of the ground. Strain and strive to the uttermost, the sailor's feet still stuck to the floor and sustained a part of his weight. The remaining portion was supported by the point of contact just under his chin. Failing to swing him clear, Kent clung on, resolved to slowly throttle him or force him to tell what he had done with the hoard. But the Man with the Gash would not throttle. Five, ten, fifteen minutes passed, and at the end of that time, in despair, Kent let his prisoner down.

"Well," he remarked, wiping away the sweat, "if you won't hang you'll shoot. Some men wasn't born to be hanged, anyway."

"An' it's a pretty mess as you'll make o' this 'ere cabin floor." Cardegee was fighting for time. "Now, look 'ere, I'll tell you wot we do; we'll lay our 'eads 'longside an' reason together. You've lost some dust. You say as 'ow I know, an' I say as 'ow I don't. Let's get a hobservation an' shape a course—"

70

"Vast heavin'!" Kent dashed in, maliciously imitating the other's enunciation. "I'm going to shape all the courses of this shebang, and you observe; and if you do anything more, I'll bore you as sure as Moses!"

"For the sake of my mother—"

"Whom God have mercy upon if she loves you. Ah! Would you?" He frustrated a hostile move on the part of the other by pressing the cold muzzle against his forehead. "Lay quiet, now! If you lift as much as a hair, you'll get it."

It was rather an awkward task, with the trigger of the gun always within pulling distance of the finger; but Kent was a weaver, and in a few minutes had the sailor tied hand and foot. Then he dragged him without and laid him by the side of the cabin, where he could overlook the river and watch the sun climb to the meridian.

"Now I'll give you till noon, and then—"

"Wot?"

"You'll be hitting the brimstone trail. But if you speak up, I'll keep you till the next bunch of mounted police come by."

"Well, Gawd blime me, if this ain't a go! 'Ere I be, innercent as a lamb, an' 'ere you be, lost all o' your top 'amper an' out o' your reckonin', run me foul an' goin' to rake me into 'ell-fire. You bloomin' old pirut! You—"

Jim Cardegee loosed the strings of his profanity and fairly outdid himself. Jacob Kent brought out a stool that he might enjoy it in comfort. Having exhausted all the possible combinations of his vocabulary, the sailor quieted down to hard thinking, his eyes constantly gauging the progress of the sun, which tore up the eastern slope of the heavens with unseemly haste. His dogs, surprised that they had not long since been put to harness, crowded around him. His helplessness appealed to the brutes. They felt that

71

something was wrong, though they knew not what, and they crowded about, howling their mournful sympathy.

"Chook! Mush-on! you Siwashes!" he cried, attempting, in a vermicular way, to kick at them, and discovering himself to be tottering on the edge of a declivity. As soon as the animals had scattered, he devoted himself to the significance of that declivity which he felt to be there but could not see. Nor was he long in arriving at a correct conclusion. In the nature of things, he figured, man is lazy. He does no more than he has to. When he builds a cabin he must put dirt on the roof. From these premises it was logical that he should carry that dirt no further than was absolutely necessary. Therefore, he lay upon the edge of the hole from which the dirt had been taken to roof Jacob Kent's cabin. This knowledge, properly utilized, might prolong things, he thought; and he then turned his attention to the moose-hide thongs which bound him. His hands were tied behind him, and pressing against the snow, they were wet with the contact. This moistening of the raw-hide he knew would tend to make it stretch, and, without apparent effort, he endeavored to stretch it more and more.

He watched the trail hungrily, and when in the direction of Sixty Mile a dark speck appeared for a moment against the white background of an ice-jam, he cast an anxious eye at the sun. It had climbed nearly to the zenith. Now and again he caught the black speck clearing the hills of ice and sinking into the intervening hollows; but he dared not permit himself more than the most cursory glances for fear of rousing his enemy's suspicion. Once, when Jacob Kent rose to his feet and searched the trail with care, Cardegee was frightened, but the dog-sled had struck a piece of trail running parallel with a jam, and remained out of sight till the danger was past.

"I'll see you 'ung for this," Cardegee threatened, attempting to draw the other's attention. "An' you'll rot in 'ell, jes' you see if you don't.

"I say," he cried, after another pause; "d'ye b'lieve in ghosts?" Kent's sudden start made him sure of his ground, and he went on: "Now a ghost 'as the right to 'aunt a man wot don't do wot he says; and you can't shuffle me off till eight bells—wot I mean is twelve o'clock—can you? 'Cos if you do, it'll 'appen as 'ow I'll 'aunt you. D'ye 'ear? A minute, a second too quick, an' I'll 'aunt you, so 'elp me, I will!"

Jacob Kent looked dubious, but declined to talk.

"'Ow's your chronometer? Wot's your longitude? 'Ow do you know as your time's correct?" Cardegee persisted, vainly hoping to beat his executioner out of a few minutes. "Is it Barrack's time you 'ave, or is it the Company time? 'Cos if you do it before the stroke o' the bell, I'll not rest. I give you fair warnin'. I'll come back. An' if you 'aven't the time, 'ow will you know? That's wot I want—'ow will you tell?"

"I'll send you off all right," Kent replied. "Got a sun-dial here."

"No good. Thirty-two degrees variation o' the needle."

"Stakes are all set."

"'Ow did you set 'em? Compass?"

"No; lined them up with the North Star."

"Sure?"

"Sure."

Cardegee groaned, then stole a glance at the trail. The sled was just clearing a rise, barely a mile away, and the dogs were in full lope, running lightly.

"'Ow close is the shadows to the line?"

Kent walked to the primitive timepiece and studied it. "Three inches," he announced, after a careful survey.

"Say, jes' sing out 'eight bells' afore you pull the gun, will you?"

Kent agreed, and they lapsed into silence. The thongs about Cardegee's wrists were slowly stretching, and he had begun to work them over his hands.

"Say, 'ow close is the shadows?"

"One inch."

The sailor wriggled slightly to assure himself that he would topple over at the right moment, and slipped the first turn over his hands.

"'Ow close?"

"Half an inch." Just then Kent heard the jarring churn of the runners and turned his eyes to the trail. The driver was lying flat on the sled and the dogs swinging down the straight stretch to the cabin. Kent whirled back, bringing his rifle to shoulder.

"It ain't eight bells yet!" Cardegee expostulated. "I'll 'aunt you, sure!"

Jacob Kent faltered. He was standing by the sun-dial, perhaps ten paces from his victim. The man on the sled must have seen that something unusual was taking place, for he had risen to his knees, his whip singing viciously among the dogs.

The shadows swept into line. Kent looked along the sights.

"Make ready!" he commanded solemnly. "Eight b—"

But just a fraction of a second too soon, Cardegee rolled backward into the hole. Kent held his fire and ran to the edge. Bang! The gun exploded full in the sailor's face as he rose to his feet. But no smoke came from the muzzle; instead, a sheet of flame burst from the side of the barrel near its butt, and Jacob Kent went down. The dogs dashed up the bank, dragging the sled over his body, and the driver sprang off as Jim Cardegee freed his hands and drew himself from the hole.

"Jim!" The new-comer recognized him. "What's the matter?"

"Wot's the matter? Oh, nothink at all. It jest 'appens as I do little things like this for my 'ealth. Wot's the matter, you bloomin' idjit? Wot's the matter, eh? Cast me loose or I'll show you wot! 'Urry up, or I'll 'olystone the decks with you!"

"Huh!" he added, as the other went to work with his sheath-knife. "Wot's the matter? I want to know. Jes' tell me that, will you, wot's the matter? Hey?"

Kent was quite dead when they rolled him over. The gun, an old-fashioned, heavy-weighted muzzle-loader, lay near him. Steel and wood had parted company. Near the butt of the right-hand barrel, with lips pressed outward, gaped a fissure several inches in length. The sailor picked it up, curiously. A glittering stream of yellow dust ran out through the crack. The facts of the case dawned upon Jim Cardegee.

"Strike me standin'!" he roared; "'ere's a go! 'Ere's 'is bloomin' dust! Gawd blime me, an' you, too, Charley, if you don't run an' get the dish-pan!"

JAN, THE UNREPENTANT

"For there's never a law of God or man Runs north of Fifty-three."

Jan rolled over, clawing and kicking. He was fighting hand and foot now, and he fought grimly, silently. Two of the three men who hung upon him, shouted directions to each other, and strove to curb the short, hairy devil who would not curb. The third man howled. His finger was between Jan's teeth.

"Quit yer tantrums, Jan, an' ease up!" panted Red Bill, getting a strangle-hold on Jan's neck. "Why on earth can't yeh hang decent and peaceable?"

But Jan kept his grip on the third man's finger, and squirmed over the floor of the tent, into the pots and pans.

"Youah no gentleman, suh," reproved Mr. Taylor, his body following his finger, and endeavoring to accommodate itself to every jerk of Jan's head. "You hev killed Mistah Gordon, as brave and honorable a gentleman as ever hit the trail aftah the dogs. Youah a murderah, suh, and without honah."

"An' yer no comrade," broke in Red Bill. "If you was, you'd hang 'thout rampin' around an' roarin'. Come on, Jan, there's a good fellow. Don't give us no more trouble. Jes' quit, an' we'll hang yeh neat and handy, an' be done with it."

"Steady, all!" Lawson, the sailorman, bawled. "Jam his head into the bean pot and batten down."

"But my fingah, suh," Mr. Taylor protested.

"Leggo with y'r finger, then! Always in the way!"

"But I can't, Mistah Lawson. It's in the critter's gullet, and nigh chewed off as 't is."

"Stand by for stays!" As Lawson gave the warning, Jan half lifted himself, and the struggling quartet floundered across the tent into a muddle of furs and blankets. In its passage it cleared the body of a man, who lay motionless, bleeding from a bullet-wound in the neck.

All this was because of the madness which had come upon Jan—the madness which comes upon a man who has stripped off the raw skin of earth and grovelled long in primal nakedness, and before whose eyes rises the fat vales of the homeland, and into whose nostrils steals the whiff of bay, and grass, and flower, and new-turned soil. Through five frigid years Jan had sown the seed. Stuart River, Forty Mile, Circle City, Koyokuk, Kotzebue, had marked his bleak and strenuous agriculture, and now it was Nome that bore the harvest,—not the Nome of golden beaches and ruby sands, but the Nome of '97, before Anvil City was located, or Eldorado District organized. John Gordon was a Yankee, and should have known better. But he passed the sharp word at a time when Jan's blood-shot eyes blazed and his teeth gritted in torment. And because of this, there was a smell of saltpetre in the tent, and one lay quietly, while the other fought like a cornered rat, and refused to hang in the decent and peacable manner suggested by his comrades.

"If you will allow me, Mistah Lawson, befoah we go further in this rumpus, I would say it wah a good idea to pry this hyer varmint's teeth apart. Neither will he bite off, nor will he let go. He has the wisdom of the sarpint, suh, the wisdom of the sarpint."

"Lemme get the hatchet to him!" vociferated the sailor.

"Lemme get the hatchet!" He shoved the steel edge close to Mr. Taylor's finger and used the man's teeth as a fulcrum. Jan held on and breathed through his nose, snorting like a grampus. "Steady, all! Now she takes it!"

"Thank you, suh; it is a powerful relief." And Mr. Taylor proceeded to gather into his arms the victim's wildly waving legs.

But Jan upreared in his Berserker rage; bleeding, frothing, cursing; five frozen years thawing into sudden hell. They swayed backward and forward, panted, sweated, like some cyclopean, many-legged monster rising from the lower deeps. The slush-lamp went over, drowned in its own fat, while the midday twilight scarce percolated through the dirty canvas of the tent.

"For the love of Gawd, Jan, get yer senses back!" pleaded Red Bill. "We ain't goin' to hurt yeh, 'r kill yeh, 'r anythin' of that sort. Jes' want to hang yeh, that's all, an' you a-messin' round an' rampagin' somethin' terrible. To think of travellin' trail together an' then bein' treated this-a way. Wouldn't 'bleeved it of yeh, Jan!"

"He's got too much steerage-way. Grab holt his legs, Taylor, and heave'm over!"

"Yes, suh, Mistah Lawson. Do you press youah weight above, after I give the word." The Kentuckian groped about him in the murky darkness. "Now, suh, now is the accepted time!"

There was a great surge, and a quarter of a ton of human flesh tottered and crashed to its fall against the side-wall. Pegs drew and guy-ropes parted, and the tent, collapsing, wrapped the battle in its greasy folds.

"Yer only makin' it harder fer yerself," Red Bill continued, at the same time driving both his thumbs into a hairy throat, the possessor of which he had pinned down. "You've made nuisance enough a' ready, an' it'll take half the day to get things straightened when we've strung yeh up."

"I'll thank you to leave go, suh," spluttered Mr. Taylor.

Red Bill grunted and loosed his grip, and the twain crawled out into the open. At the same instant Jan kicked clear of the sailor, and took to his heels across the snow.

"Hi! you lazy devils! Buck! Bright! Sic'm! Pull 'm down!" sang out Lawson, lunging through the snow after the fleeing man. Buck and Bright, followed by the rest of the dogs, outstripped him and rapidly overhauled the murderer.

There was no reason that these men should do this; no reason for Jan to run away; no reason for them to attempt to prevent him. On the one hand stretched the barren snow-land; on the other, the frozen sea. With neither food nor shelter, he could not run far. All they had to do was to wait till he wandered back to the tent, as he inevitably must, when the frost and hunger laid hold of him. But these men did not stop to think. There was a certain taint of madness running in the veins of all of them. Besides, blood had been spilled, and upon them was the blood-lust, thick and hot. "Vengeance is mine," saith the Lord, and He saith it in temperate climes where the warm sun steals away the energies of men. But in the Northland they have discovered that prayer is only efficacious when backed by muscle, and they are accustomed to doing things for themselves. God is everywhere, they have heard, but he flings a shadow over the land for half the year that they may not find him; so they grope in darkness, and it is not to be wondered that they often doubt, and deem the Decalogue out of gear.

Jan ran blindly, reckoning not of the way of his feet, for he was mastered by the verb "to live." To live! To exist! Buck flashed gray through the air, but missed. The man struck madly at him, and stumbled. Then the white teeth of Bright closed on his mackinaw jacket, and he pitched into the snow. *To live! To exist!* He fought wildly as ever, the centre

79

of a tossing heap of men and dogs. His left hand gripped a wolf-dog by the scruff of the back, while the arm was passed around the neck of Lawson. Every struggle of the dog helped to throttle the hapless sailor. Jan's right hand was buried deep in the curling tendrils of Red Bill's shaggy head, and beneath all, Mr. Taylor lay pinned and helpless. It was a deadlock, for the strength of his madness was prodigious; but suddenly, without apparent reason, Jan loosed his various grips and rolled over quietly on his back. His adversaries drew away a little, dubious and disconcerted. Jan grinned viciously.

"Mine friends," he said, still grinning, "you haf asked me to be politeful, und now I am politeful. Vot piziness vood you do mit me?"

"That's right, Jan. Be ca'm," soothed Red Bill. "I knowed you'd come to yer senses afore long. Jes' be ca'm now, an' we'll do the trick with neatness and despatch."

"Vot piziness? Vot trick?"

"The hangin'. An' yeh oughter thank yer lucky stars for havin' a man what knows his business. I've did it afore now, more'n once, down in the States, an' I can do it to a T."

"Hang who? Me?"

"Yep."

"Ha! ha! Shust hear der man speak foolishness! Gif me a hand, Bill, und I vill get up und be hung." He crawled stiffly to his feet and looked about him. "Herr Gott! listen to der man! He vood hang me! Ho! ho! ho! I tank not! Yes, I tank not!"

"And I tank yes, you swab," Lawson spoke up mockingly, at the same time cutting a sled-lashing and coiling it up with ominous care. "Judge Lynch holds court this day."

80

"Von liddle while." Jan stepped back from the proffered noose. "I haf somedings to ask und to make der great proposition. Kentucky, you know about der Shudge Lynch?"

"Yes, suh. It is an institution of free men and of gentlemen, and it is an ole one and time-honored. Corruption may wear the robe of magistracy, suh, but Judge Lynch can always be relied upon to give justice without court fees. I repeat, suh, without court fees. Law may be bought and sold, but in this enlightened land justice is free as the air we breathe, strong as the licker we drink, prompt as—"

"Cut it short! Find out what the beggar wants," interrupted Lawson, spoiling the peroration.

"Vell, Kentucky, tell me dis: von man kill von odder man, Shudge Lynch hang dot man?"

"If the evidence is strong enough—yes, suh."

"An' the evidence in this here case is strong enough to hang a dozen men, Jan," broke in Red Bill.

"Nefer you mind, Bill. I talk mit you next. Now von anodder ding I ask Kentucky. If Shudge Lynch hang not der man, vot den?"

"If Judge Lynch does not hang the man, then the man goes free, and his hands are washed clean of blood. And further, suh, our great and glorious constitution has said, to wit: that no man may twice be placed in jeopardy of his life for one and the same crime, or words to that effect."

"Unt dey can't shoot him, or hit him mit a club over der head alongside, or do nodings more mit him?"

"No, suh."

"Goot! You hear vot Kentucky speaks, all you noddleheads?

81

Now I talk mit Bill. You know der piziness, Bill, und you hang me up brown, eh? Vot you say?"

"'Betcher life, an', Jan, if yeh don't give no more trouble ye'll be almighty proud of the job. I'm a connesoor."

"You haf der great head, Bill, und know somedings or two. Und you know two und one makes tree—ain't it?"

Bill nodded.

"Und when you haf two dings, you haf not tree dings—ain't it? Now you follow mit me close und I show you. It takes tree dings to hang. First ding, you haf to haf der man. Goot! I am der man. Second ding, you haf to haf der rope. Lawson haf der rope. Goot! Und tird ding, you haf to haf someding to tie der rope to. Sling your eyes over der landscape und find der tird ding to tie der rope to? Eh? Vot you say?"

Mechanically they swept the ice and snow with their eyes. It was a homogeneous scene, devoid of contrasts or bold contours, dreary, desolate, and monotonous,—the ice-packed sea, the slow slope of the beach, the background of low-lying hills, and over all thrown the endless mantle of snow. "No trees, no bluffs, no cabins, no telegraph poles, nothin'," moaned Red Bill; "nothin' respectable enough nor big enough to swing the toes of a five-foot man clear o' the ground. I give it up." He looked yearningly at that portion of Jan's anatomy which joins the head and shoulders. "Give it up," he repeated sadly to Lawson. "Throw the rope down. Gawd never intended this here country for livin' purposes, an' that's a cold frozen fact."

Jan grinned triumphantly. "I tank I go mit der tent und haf a smoke."

"Ostensiblee y'r correct, Bill, me son," spoke up Lawson; "but y'r a dummy, and you can lay to that for another cold frozen fact. Takes a sea farmer to learn you landsmen things. Ever hear of a pair of shears? Then clap y'r eyes to this."

The sailor worked rapidly. From the pile of dunnage where they had pulled up the boat the preceding fall, he unearthed a pair of long oars. These he lashed together, at nearly right angles, close to the ends of the blades. Where the handles rested he kicked holes through the snow to the sand. At the point of intersection he attached two guy-ropes, making the end of one fast to a cake of beach-ice. The other guy he passed over to Red Bill. "Here, me son, lay holt o' that and run it out."

And to his horror, Jan saw his gallows rise in the air. "No! no!" he cried, recoiling and putting up his fists. "It is not goot! I vill not hang! Come, you noddleheads! I vill lick you, all together, von after der odder! I vill blay hell! I vill do eferydings! Und I vill die pefore I hang!"

The sailor permitted the two other men to clinch with the mad creature. They rolled and tossed about furiously, tearing up snow and tundra, their fierce struggle writing a tragedy of human passion on the white sheet spread by nature. And ever and anon a hand or foot of Jan emerged from the tangle, to be gripped by Lawson and lashed fast with rope-yarns. Pawing, clawing, blaspheming, he was conquered and bound, inch by inch, and drawn to where the inexorable shears lay like a pair of gigantic dividers on the snow. Red Bill adjusted the noose, placing the hangman's knot properly under the left ear. Mr. Taylor and Lawson tailed onto the running-guy, ready at the word to elevate the gallows. Bill lingered, contemplating his work with artistic appreciation.

"Herr Gott! Vood you look at it!"

The horror in Jan's voice caused the rest to desist. The fallen tent had uprisen, and in the gathering twilight it flapped ghostly arms about and titubated toward them drunkenly. But the next instant John Gordon found the opening and crawled forth.

"What the flaming—!" For the moment his voice died away in his throat as his eyes took in the tableau. "Hold on! I'm not dead!" he cried out, coming up to the group with stormy countenance.

"Allow me, Mistah Gordon, to congratulate you upon youah escape," Mr. Taylor ventured. "A close shave, suh, a powahful close shave."

" Congratulate hell! I might have been dead and rotten and no thanks to you, you—!" And thereat John Gordon delivered himself of a vigorous flood of English, terse, intensive, denunciative, and composed solely of expletives and adjectives.

"Simply creased me," he went on when he had eased himself sufficiently. "Ever crease cattle, Taylor?"

"Yes, suh, many a time down in God's country."

"Just so. That's what happened to me. Bullet just grazed the base of my skull at the top of the neck. Stunned me but no harm done." He turned to the bound man. "Get up, Jan. I'm going to lick you to a standstill or you're going to apologize. The rest of you lads stand clear."

"I tank not. Shust tie me loose und you see," replied Jan, the Unrepentant, the devil within him still unconquered. "Und after as I lick you, I take der rest of der noddleheads, von after der odder, altogedder!"

GRIT OF WOMEN

A wolfish head, wistful-eyed and frost-rimed, thrust aside the tent-flaps.

"Hi! Chook! Siwash! Chook, you limb of Satan!" chorused the protesting inmates. Bettles rapped the dog sharply with a tin plate, and it withdrew hastily. Louis Savoy refastened the flaps, kicked a frying-pan over against the bottom, and warmed his hands. It was very cold without. Forty-eight hours gone, the spirit thermometer had burst at sixty-eight below, and since that time it had grown steadily and bitterly colder. There was no telling when the snap would end. And it is poor policy, unless the gods will it, to venture far from a stove at such times, or to increase the quantity of cold atmosphere one must breathe. Men sometimes do it, and sometimes they chill their lungs. This leads up to a dry, hacking cough, noticeably irritable when bacon is being fried. After that, somewhere along in the spring or summer, a hole is burned in the frozen muck. Into this a man's carcass is dumped, covered over with moss, and left with the assurance that it will rise on the crack of Doom, wholly and frigidly intact. For those of little faith, sceptical of material integration on that fateful day, no fitter country than the Klondike can be recommended to die in. But it is not to be inferred from this that it is a fit country for living purposes.

It was very cold without, but it was not over-warm within. The only article which might be designated furniture was the stove, and for this the men were frank in displaying their preference. Upon half of the floor pine boughs had been cast; above this were spread the sleeping-furs, beneath lay the winter's snowfall. The remainder of the floor was moccasin-packed snow, littered with pots and pans and the general *impedimenta* of an Arctic camp. The stove was red

85

and roaring hot, but only a bare three feet away lay a block of ice, as sharp-edged and dry as when first quarried from the creek bottom. The pressure of the outside cold forced the inner heat upward. Just above the stove, where the pipe penetrated the roof, was a tiny circle of dry canvas; next, with the pipe always as centre, a circle of steaming canvas; next a damp and moisture-exuding ring; and finally, the rest of the tent, sidewalls and top, coated with a half-inch of dry, white, crystal-encrusted frost.

"*Oh!* OH! OH!" A young fellow, lying asleep in the furs, bearded and wan and weary, raised a moan of pain, and without waking increased the pitch and intensity of his anguish. His body half-lifted from the blankets, and quivered and shrank spasmodically, as though drawing away from a bed of nettles.

"Roll'm over!" ordered Bettles. "He's crampin'."

And thereat, with pitiless good-will, he was pitched upon and rolled and thumped and pounded by half-a-dozen willing comrades.

"Damn the trail," he muttered softly, as he threw off the robes and sat up. "I've run across country, played quarter three seasons hand-running, and hardened myself in all manner of ways; and then I pilgrim it into this God-forsaken land and find myself an effeminate Athenian without the simplest rudiments of manhood!" He hunched up to the fire and rolled a cigarette. "Oh, I'm not whining. I can take my medicine all right, all right; but I'm just decently ashamed of myself, that's all. Here I am, on top of a dirty thirty miles, as knocked up and stiff and sore as a pink-tea degenerate after a five-mile walk on a country turn-pike. Bah! It makes me sick! Got a match?" "Don't git the tantrums, youngster." Bettles passed over the required fire-stick and waxed patriarchal. "Ye've gotter 'low some for the breakin'-in. Sufferin' cracky! don't I recollect the first time I hit the trail! Stiff? I've seen the time it'd take me ten minutes to git my mouth from the water-hole an' come to my feet—every jint crackin' an' kickin' fit to kill. Cramp? In sech knots it'd take the camp half a day to untangle me. You're all right, for a cub, any ye've the true sperrit. Come this day year, you'll walk all us old bucks into the ground any time. An' best in your favor, you hain't got that streak of fat in your make-up which has sent many a husky man to the bosom of Abraham afore his right and proper time."

"Streak of fat?"

"Yep. Comes along of bulk. 'T ain't the big men as is the best when it comes to the trail."

"Never heard of it."

"Never heered of it, eh? Well, it's a dead straight, open-an'-shut fact, an' no gittin' round. Bulk's all well enough for a mighty big effort, but 'thout stayin' powers it ain't worth a continental whoop; an' stayin' powers an' bulk ain't runnin' mates. Takes the small, wiry fellows when it comes to gittin' right down an' hangin' on like a lean-jowled dog to a bone. Why, hell's fire, the big men they ain't in it!"

"By gar!" broke in Louis Savoy, "dat is no, vot you call, josh! I know one mans, so vaire beeg like ze buffalo. Wit him, on ze Sulphur Creek stampede, go one small mans, Lon McFane. You know dat Lon McFane, dat leetle Irisher wit ze red hair and ze grin. An' dey walk an' walk an' walk, all ze day long an' ze night long. And beeg mans, him become vaire tired, an' lay down mooch in ze snow. And leetle mans keek beeg mans, an' him cry like, vot you call—ah! vot you call ze kid. And leetle mans keek an' keek an' keek, an' bime by, long time, long way, keek beeg mans into my cabin. Tree days 'fore him crawl out my blankets. Nevaire I see beeg squaw like him. No nevaire. Him haf vot you call ze streak of fat. You bet."

"But there was Axel Gunderson," Prince spoke up. The great Scandinavian, with the tragic events which shadowed his passing, had made a deep mark on the mining engineer. "He lies up there, somewhere." He swept his hand in the vague direction of the mysterious east.

"Biggest man that ever turned his heels to Salt Water, or run a moose down with sheer grit," supplemented Bettles; "but he's the prove-the-rule exception. Look at his woman, Unga,—tip the scales at a hundred an' ten, clean meat an' nary ounce to spare. She'd bank grit 'gainst his for all there was in him, an' see him, an' go him better if it was possible. Nothing over the earth, or in it, or under it, she wouldn't 'a' done."

"But she loved him," objected the engineer.

"'T ain't that. It—"

"Look you, brothers," broke in Sitka Charley from his seat on the grub-box. "Ye have spoken of the streak of fat that runs in big men's muscles, of the grit of women and the love, and ye have spoken fair; but I have in mind things which happened when the land was young and the fires of men apart as the stars. It was then I had concern with a big man, and a streak of fat, and a woman. And the woman was small; but her heart was greater than the beef-heart of the man, and she had grit. And we traveled a weary trail, even to the Salt Water, and the cold was bitter, the snow deep, the hunger great. And the woman's love was a mighty love—no more can man say than this."

He paused, and with the hatchet broke pieces of ice from the large chunk beside him. These he threw into the gold pan on the stove, where the drinking-water thawed. The men drew up closer, and he of the cramps sought greater comfort vainly for his stiffened body.

"Brothers, my blood is red with Siwash, but my heart is white. To the faults of my fathers I owe the one, to the virtues of my friends the other. A great truth came to me when I was yet a boy. I learned that to your kind and you was given the earth; that the Siwash could not withstand you, and like the caribou and the bear, must perish in the cold. So I came into the warm and sat among you, by your fires, and behold, I became one of you, I have seen much in my time. I have known strange things, and bucked big, on big trails, with men of many breeds. And because of these things, I measure deeds after your manner, and judge men, and think thoughts. Wherefore, when I speak harshly of one of your own kind, I know you will not take it amiss; and when I speak high of one of my father's people, you will not take it upon you to say, 'Sitka Charley is Siwash, and there is a crooked light in his eyes and small honor to his tongue.' Is it not so?"

Deep down in throat, the circle vouchsafed its assent.

"The woman was Passuk. I got her in fair trade from her people, who were of the Coast and whose Chilcat totem stood at the head of a salt arm of the sea. My heart did not go out to the woman, nor did I take stock of her looks. For she scarce took her eyes from the ground, and she was timid and afraid, as girls will be when cast into a stranger's arms whom they have never seen before. As I say, there was no place in my heart for her to creep, for I had a great journey in mind, and stood in need of one to feed my dogs and to lift a paddle with me through the long river days. One blanket would cover the twain; so I chose Passuk.

"Have I not said I was a servant to the Government? If not, it is well that ye know. So I was taken on a warship, sleds and dogs and evaporated foods, and with me came Passuk. And we went north, to the winter ice-rim of Bering Sea, where we were landed,—myself, and Passuk, and the dogs. I was also given moneys of the Government, for I was its servant, and charts of lands which the eyes of man had never dwelt upon, and messages. These messages were sealed, and protected shrewdly from the weather, and I was to deliver them to the whale-ships of the Arctic, ice-bound by the great Mackenzie. Never was there so great a river, forgetting only our own Yukon, the Mother of all Rivers.

"All of which is neither here nor there, for my story deals not with the whale-ships, nor the berg-bound winter I spent by the Mackenzie. Afterward, in the spring, when the days lengthened and there was a crust to the snow, we came south, Passuk and I, to the Country of the Yukon. A weary journey, but the sun pointed out the way of our feet. It was a naked land then, as I have said, and we worked up the current, with pole and paddle, till we came to Forty Mile. Good it was to see white faces once again, so we put into the bank. And that winter was a hard winter. The darkness and the cold drew down upon us, and with them the famine. To each man the agent of the Company gave forty pounds of flour and twenty of bacon. There were no beans. And, the dogs howled always, and there were flat bellies and deep-lined faces, and strong men became weak, and weak men died. There was also much scurvy.

"Then came we together in the store one night, and the empty shelves made us feel our own emptiness the more. We talked low, by the light of the fire, for the candles had been set aside for those who might yet gasp in the spring. Discussion was held, and it was said that a man must go forth to the Salt Water and tell to the world our misery. At this all eyes turned to me, for it was understood that I was a great traveler. 'It is seven hundred miles,' said I, 'to Haines Mission by the sea, and every inch of it snowshoe work. Give me the pick of your dogs and the best of your grub, and I will go. And with me shall go Passuk.'

"To this they were agreed. But there arose one, Long Jeff, a Yankee-man, big-boned and big-muscled. Also his talk was big. He, too, was a mighty traveler, he said, born to the snowshoe and bred up on buffalo milk. He would go with me, in case I fell by the trail, that he might carry the word on to the Mission. I was young, and I knew not Yankee-men. How was I to know that big talk betokened the streak of fat, or that Yankee-men who did great things kept their teeth together? So we took the pick of the dogs and the best of the grub, and struck the trail, we three,—Passuk, Long Jeff, and I.

"Well, ye have broken virgin snow, labored at the gee-pole, and are not unused to the packed river-jams; so I will talk little of the toil, save that on some days we made ten miles, and on others thirty, but more often ten. And the best of the grub was not good, while we went on stint from the start. Likewise the pick of the dogs was poor, and we were hard put to keep them on their legs. At the White River our three sleds became two sleds, and we had only come two hundred miles. But we lost nothing; the dogs that left the traces went into the bellies of those that remained.

"Not a greeting, not a curl of smoke, till we made Pelly. Here I had counted on grub; and here I had counted on leaving Long Jeff, who was whining and trail-sore. But the factor's lungs were wheezing, his eyes bright, his cache nigh empty; and he showed us the empty cache of the missionary, also his grave with the rocks piled high to keep off the dogs. There was a bunch of Indians there, but babies and old men there were none, and it was clear that few would see the spring.

"So we pulled on, light-stomached and heavy-hearted, with half a thousand miles of snow and silence between us and Haines Mission by the sea. The darkness was at its worst, and at midday the sun could not clear the sky-line to the south. But the ice-jams were smaller, the going better; so I pushed the dogs hard and traveled late and early. As I said at Forty Mile, every inch of it was snow-shoe work. And the shoes made great sores on our feet, which cracked and scabbed but would not heal. And every day these sores grew more grievous, till in the morning, when we girded on the shoes, Long Jeff cried like a child. I put him at the fore of the light sled to break trail, but he slipped off the shoes for comfort. Because of this the trail was not packed, his moccasins made great holes, and into these holes the dogs wallowed. The bones of the dogs were ready to break through their hides, and this was not good for them. So I spoke hard words to the man, and he promised, and broke his word. Then I beat him with the dog-whip, and after that the dogs wallowed no more. He was a child, what of the pain and the streak of fat.

"But Passuk. While the man lay by the fire and wept, she cooked, and in the morning helped lash the sleds, and in the evening to unlash them. And she saved the dogs. Ever was she to the fore, lifting the webbed shoes and making the way easy. Passuk—how shall I say?—I took it for granted that she should do these things, and thought no more about it. For my mind was busy with other matters, and besides, I was young in years and knew little of woman. It was only on looking back that I came to understand.

"And the man became worthless. The dogs had little strength in them, but he stole rides on the sled when he lagged behind. Passuk said she would take the one sled, so the man had nothing to do. In the morning I gave him his fair share of grub and started him on the trail alone. Then the woman and I broke camp, packed the sleds, and harnessed the dogs. By midday, when the sun mocked us, we would overtake the man, with the tears frozen on his cheeks, and pass him. In the night we made camp, set aside his fair share of grub, and spread his furs. Also we made a big fire, that he might see. And hours afterward he would come limping in, and eat his grub with moans and groans, and sleep. He was not sick, this man. He was only trail-sore and tired, and weak with hunger. But Passuk and I were trail-sore and tired, and weak with hunger; and we did all the work and he did none. But he had the streak of fat of which our brother Bettles has spoken. Further, we gave the man always his fair share of grub.

"Then one day we met two ghosts journeying through the Silence. They were a man and a boy, and they were white. The ice had opened on Lake Le Barge, and through it had gone their main outfit. One blanket each carried about his shoulders. At night they built a fire and crouched over it till morning. They had a little flour. This they stirred in warm water and drank. The man showed me eight cups of flour—all they had, and Pelly, stricken with famine, two hundred miles away. They said, also, that there was an Indian behind; that they had whacked fair, but that he could not keep up. I did not believe they had whacked fair, else would the Indian have kept up. But I could give them no grub. They strove to steal a dog—the fattest, which was very thin—but I shoved my pistol in their faces and told them begone. And they went away, like drunken men, through the Silence toward Pelly.

"I had three dogs now, and one sled, and the dogs were only bones and hair. When there is little wood, the fire burns low and the cabin grows cold. So with us. With little grub the frost bites sharp, and our faces were black and frozen till our own mothers would not have known us. And our feet were very sore. In the morning, when I hit the trail, I sweated to keep down the cry when the pain of the snowshoes smote me. Passuk never opened her lips, but stepped to the fore to break the way. The man howled.

"The Thirty Mile was swift, and the current ate away the ice from beneath, and there were many air-holes and cracks, and much open water. One day we came upon the man, resting, for he had gone ahead, as was his wont, in the morning. But between us was open water. This he had passed around by taking to the rim-ice where it was too narrow for a sled. So we found an ice-bridge. Passuk weighed little, and went first, with a long pole crosswise in her hands in chance she broke through. But she was light, and her shoes large, and she passed over. Then she called the dogs. But they had neither poles nor shoes, and they broke through and were swept under by the water. I held tight to the sled from behind, till the traces broke and the dogs went on down under the ice. There was little meat to them, but I had counted on them for a week's grub, and they were gone.

"The next morning I divided all the grub, which was little, into three portions. And I told Long Jeff that he could keep up with us, or not, as he saw fit; for we were going to travel light and fast. But he raised his voice and cried over his sore

93

feet and his troubles, and said harsh things against comradeship. Passuk's feet were sore, and my feet were sore—ay, sorer than his, for we had worked with the dogs; also, we looked to see. Long Jeff swore he would die before he hit the trail again; so Passuk took a fur robe, and I a cooking pot and an axe, and we made ready to go. But she looked on the man's portion, and said, 'It is wrong to waste good food on a baby. He is better dead.' I shook my head and said no—that a comrade once was a comrade always. Then she spoke of the men of Forty Mile; that they were many men and good; and that they looked to me for grub in the spring. But when I still said no, she snatched the pistol from my belt, quick, and as our brother Bettles has spoken, Long Jeff went to the bosom of Abraham before his time. I chided Passuk for this; but she showed no sorrow, nor was she sorrowful. And in my heart I knew she was right."

Sitka Charley paused and threw pieces of ice into the gold pan on the stove. The men were silent, and their backs chilled to the sobbing cries of the dogs as they gave tongue to their misery in the outer cold.

"And day by day we passed in the snow the sleeping-places of the two ghosts—Passuk and I—and we knew we would be glad for such ere we made Salt Water. Then we came to the Indian, like another ghost, with his face set toward Pelly. They had not whacked up fair, the man and the boy, he said, and he had had no flour for three days. Each night he boiled pieces of his moccasins in a cup, and ate them. He did not have much moccasins left. And he was a Coast Indian, and told us these things through Passuk, who talked his tongue. He was a stranger in the Yukon, and he knew not the way, but his face was set to Pelly. How far was it? Two sleeps? ten? a hundred—he did not know, but he was going to Pelly. It was too far to turn back; he could only keep on.

"He did not ask for grub, for he could see we, too, were hard put. Passuk looked at the man, and at me, as though she were of two minds, like a mother partridge whose young are in trouble. So I turned to her and said, 'This man has been dealt unfair. Shall I give him of our grub a portion?' I saw her eyes light, as with quick pleasure; but she looked long at the man and at me, and her mouth drew close and hard, and she said, 'No. The Salt Water is afar off, and Death lies in wait. Better it is that he take this stranger man and let my man Charley pass.' So the man went away in the Silence toward Pelly. That night she wept. Never had I seen her weep before. Nor was it the smoke of the fire, for the wood was dry wood. So I marveled at her sorrow, and thought her woman's heart had grown soft at the darkness of the trail and the pain.

"Life is a strange thing. Much have I thought on it, and pondered long, yet daily the strangeness of it grows not less, but more. Why this longing for Life? It is a game which no man wins. To live is to toil hard, and to suffer sore, till Old Age creeps heavily upon us and we throw down our hands on the cold ashes of dead fires. It is hard to live. In pain the babe sucks his first breath, in pain the old man gasps his last, and all his days are full of trouble and sorrow; yet he goes down to the open arms of Death, stumbling, falling, with head turned backward, fighting to the last. And Death is kind. It is only Life, and the things of Life that hurt. Yet we love Life, and we hate Death. It is very strange.

"We spoke little, Passuk and I, in the days which came. In the night we lay in the snow like dead people, and in the morning we went on our way, walking like dead people. And all things were dead. There were no ptarmigan, no squirrels, no snowshoe rabbits,—nothing. The river made no sound beneath its white robes. The sap was frozen in the forest. And it became cold, as now; and in the night the stars drew near and large, and leaped and danced; and in the day the sun-dogs mocked us till we saw many suns, and all the air flashed and sparkled, and the snow was diamond dust. And there was no heat, no sound, only the bitter cold and the Silence. As I say, we walked like dead people, as in a dream, and we kept no count of time. Only our faces were set to Salt Water, our souls strained for Salt Water, and our feet carried us toward Salt Water. We camped by the Tahkeena, and knew it not. Our eyes looked upon the White Horse, but we saw it not. Our feet trod the portage of the Canyon, but they felt it not. We felt nothing. And we fell often by the way, but we fell, always, with our faces toward Salt Water.

"Our last grub went, and we had shared fair, Passuk and I, but she fell more often, and at Caribou Crossing her strength left her. And in the morning we lay beneath the one robe and did not take the trail. It was in my mind to stay there and meet Death hand-in-hand with Passuk; for I had grown old, and had learned the love of woman. Also, it was eighty miles to Haines Mission, and the great Chilcoot, far above the timber-line, reared his storm-swept head between. But Passuk spoke to me, low, with my ear against her lips that I might hear. And now, because she need not fear my anger, she spoke her heart, and told me of her love, and of many things which I did not understand.

"And she said: 'You are my man, Charley, and I have been a good woman to you. And in all the days I have made your fire, and cooked your food, and fed your dogs, and lifted paddle or broken trail, I have not complained. Nor did I say that there was more warmth in the lodge of my father, or that there was more grub on the Chilcat. When you have spoken, I have listened. When you have ordered, I have obeyed. Is it not so, Charley?'

"And I said: 'Ay, it is so.'

"And she said: 'When first you came to the Chilcat, nor looked upon me, but bought me as a man buys a dog, and took me away, my heart was hard against you and filled with bitterness and fear. But that was long ago. For you were kind to me, Charley, as a good man is kind to his dog. Your heart was cold, and there was no room for me; yet you dealt me fair and your ways were just. And I was with you when you did bold deeds and led great ventures, and I measured you against the men of other breeds, and I saw you stood among them full of honor, and your word was wise, your tongue true. And I grew proud of you, till it came that you

96

filled all my heart, and all my thought was of you. You were as the midsummer sun, when its golden trail runs in a circle and never leaves the sky. And whatever way I cast my eyes I beheld the sun. But your heart was ever cold, Charley, and there was no room.'

"And I said: 'It is so. It was cold, and there was no room. But that is past. Now my heart is like the snowfall in the spring, when the sun has come back. There is a great thaw and a bending, a sound of running waters, and a budding and sprouting of green things. And there is drumming of partridges, and songs of robins, and great music, for the winter is broken, Passuk, and I have learned the love of woman.'

"She smiled and moved for me to draw her closer. And she said, 'I am glad.' After that she lay quiet for a long time, breathing softly, her head upon my breast. Then she whispered: 'The trail ends here, and I am tired. But first I would speak of other things. In the long ago, when I was a girl on the Chilcat, I played alone among the skin bales of my father's lodge; for the men were away on the hunt, and the women and boys were dragging in the meat. It was in the spring, and I was alone. A great brown bear, just awake from his winter's sleep, hungry, his fur hanging to the bones in flaps of leanness, shoved his head within the lodge and said, "Oof!" My brother came running back with the first sled of meat. And he fought the bear with burning sticks from the fire, and the dogs in their harnesses, with the sled behind them, fell upon the bear. There was a great battle and much noise. They rolled in the fire, the skin bales were scattered, the lodge overthrown. But in the end the bear lay dead, with the fingers of my brother in his mouth and the marks of his claws upon my brother's face. Did you mark the Indian by the Pelly trail, his mitten which had no thumb, his hand which he warmed by our fire? He was my brother. And I said he should have no grub. And he went away in the Silence without grub.'

"This, my brothers, was the love of Passuk, who died in the

snow, by the Caribou Crossing. It was a mighty love, for she denied her brother for the man who led her away on weary trails to a bitter end. And, further, such was this woman's love, she denied herself. Ere her eyes closed for the last time she took my hand and slipped it under her squirrel-skin *parka* to her waist. I felt there a well-filled pouch, and learned the secret of her lost strength. Day by day we had shared fair, to the last least bit; and day by day but half her share had she eaten. The other half had gone into the well-filled pouch.

"And she said: 'This is the end of the trail for Passuk; but your trail, Charley, leads on and on, over the great Chilcoot, down to Haines Mission and the sea. And it leads on and on, by the light of many suns, over unknown lands and strange waters, and it is full of years and honors and great glories. It leads you to the lodges of many women, and good women, but it will never lead you to a greater love than the love of Passuk.'

"And I knew the woman spoke true. But a madness came upon me, and I threw the well-filled pouch from me, and swore that my trail had reached an end, till her tired eyes grew soft with tears, and she said: 'Among men has Sitka Charley walked in honor, and ever has his word been true. Does he forget that honor now, and talk vain words by the Caribou Crossing? Does he remember no more the men of Forty Mile, who gave him of their grub the best, of their dogs the pick? Ever has Passuk been proud of her man. Let him lift himself up, gird on his snowshoes, and begone, that she may still keep her pride.'

"And when she grew cold in my arms I arose, and sought out the well-filled pouch, and girt on my snowshoes, and staggered along the trail; for there was a weakness in my knees, and my head was dizzy, and in my ears there was a roaring, and a flashing of fire upon my eyes. The forgotten trails of boyhood came back to me. I sat by the full pots of the *potlach* feast, and raised my voice in song, and danced to the chanting of the men and maidens and the booming of the walrus drums. And Passuk held my hand and walked by my side. When I laid down to sleep, she waked me. When I stumbled and fell, she raised me. When I wandered in the deep snow, she led me back to the trail. And in this wise, like a man bereft of reason, who sees strange visions and whose thoughts are light with wine, I came to Haines Mission by the sea."

Sitka Charley threw back the tent-flaps. It was midday. To the south, just clearing the bleak Henderson Divide, poised the cold-disked sun. On either hand the sun-dogs blazed. The air was a gossamer of glittering frost. In the foreground, beside the trail, a wolf-dog, bristling with frost, thrust a long snout heavenward and mourned.

WHERE THE TRAIL FORKS

"Must I, then, must I, then, now leave this town—
And you, my love, stay here?"—*Schwabian Folk-song.*

The singer, clean-faced and cheery-eyed, bent over and
added water to a pot of simmering beans, and then, rising, a
stick of firewood in hand, drove back the circling dogs from
the grub-box and cooking-gear. He was blue of eye, and his
long hair was golden, and it was a pleasure to look upon his
lusty freshness. A new moon was thrusting a dim horn
above the white line of close-packed snow-capped pines
which ringed the camp and segregated it from all the world.
Overhead, so clear it was and cold, the stars danced with
quick, pulsating movements. To the southeast an
evanescent greenish glow heralded the opening revels of the
aurora borealis. Two men, in the immediate foreground, lay
upon the bearskin which was their bed. Between the skin
and naked snow was a six-inch layer of pine boughs. The
blankets were rolled back. For shelter, there was a fly at
their backs,—a sheet of canvas stretched between two trees
and angling at forty-five degrees. This caught the radiating
heat from the fire and flung it down upon the skin. Another
man sat on a sled, drawn close to the blaze, mending
moccasins. To the right, a heap of frozen gravel and a rude
windlass denoted where they toiled each day in dismal
groping for the pay-streak. To the left, four pairs of
snowshoes stood erect, showing the mode of travel which
obtained when the stamped snow of the camp was left
behind.

That Schwabian folk-song sounded strangely pathetic under
the cold northern stars, and did not do the men good who
lounged about the fire after the toil of the day. It put a dull
ache into their hearts, and a yearning which was akin to

belly-hunger, and sent their souls questing southward across the divides to the sun-lands.

"For the love of God, Sigmund, shut up!" expostulated one of the men. His hands were clenched painfully, but he hid them from sight in the folds of the bearskin upon which he lay.

"And what for, Dave Wertz?" Sigmund demanded. "Why shall I not sing when the heart is glad?"

"Because you've got no call to, that's why. Look about you, man, and think of the grub we've been defiling our bodies with for the last twelvemonth, and the way we've lived and worked like beasts!"

Thus abjured, Sigmund, the golden-haired, surveyed it all, and the frost-rimmed wolf-dogs and the vapor breaths of the men. "And why shall not the heart be glad?" he laughed. "It is good; it is all good. As for the grub—" He doubled up his arm and caressed the swelling biceps. "And if we have lived and worked like beasts, have we not been paid like kings? Twenty dollars to the pan the streak is running, and we know it to be eight feet thick. It is another Klondike—and we know it—Jim Hawes there, by your elbow, knows it and complains not. And there's Hitchcock! He sews moccasins like an old woman, and waits against the time. Only you can't wait and work until the wash-up in the spring. Then we shall all be rich, rich as kings, only you cannot wait. You want to go back to the States. So do I, and I was born there, but I can wait, when each day the gold in the pan shows up yellow as butter in the churning. But you want your good time, and, like a child, you cry for it now. Bah! Why shall I not sing:

"In a year, in a year, when the grapes are ripe,   I
shall stay no more away.
Then if you still are true, my love,
It will be our wedding day.
In a year, in a year, when my time is past,

Then I'll live in your love for aye.
Then if you still are true, my love,
It will be our wedding day."

The dogs, bristling and growling, drew in closer to the firelight. There was a monotonous crunch-crunch of webbed shoes, and between each crunch the dragging forward of the heel of the shoe like the sound of sifting sugar. Sigmund broke off from his song to hurl oaths and firewood at the animals. Then the light was parted by a fur-clad figure, and an Indian girl slipped out of the webs, threw back the hood of her squirrel-skin *parka*, and stood in their midst. Sigmund and the men on the bearskin greeted her as "Sipsu," with the customary "Hello," but Hitchcock made room on the sled that she might sit beside him.

"And how goes it, Sipsu?" he asked, talking, after her fashion, in broken English and bastard Chinook. "Is the hunger still mighty in the camp? and has the witch doctor yet found the cause wherefore game is scarce and no moose in the land?"

"Yes; even so. There is little game, and we prepare to eat the dogs. Also has the witch doctor found the cause of all this evil, and to-morrow will he make sacrifice and cleanse the camp."

"And what does the sacrifice chance to be?—a new-born babe or some poor devil of a squaw, old and shaky, who is a care to the tribe and better out of the way?"

"It chanced not that wise; for the need was great, and he chose none other than the chief's daughter; none other than I, Sipsu."

"Hell!" The word rose slowly to Hitchcock's lips, and brimmed over full and deep, in a way which bespoke wonder and consideration.

"Wherefore we stand by a forking of the trail, you and I," she

102

went on calmly, "and I have come that we may look once more upon each other, and once more only."

She was born of primitive stock, and primitive had been her traditions and her days; so she regarded life stoically, and human sacrifice as part of the natural order. The powers which ruled the day-light and the dark, the flood and the frost, the bursting of the bud and the withering of the leaf, were angry and in need of propitiation. This they exacted in many ways,—death in the bad water, through the treacherous ice-crust, by the grip of the grizzly, or a wasting sickness which fell upon a man in his own lodge till he coughed, and the life of his lungs went out through his mouth and nostrils. Likewise did the powers receive sacrifice. It was all one. And the witch doctor was versed in the thoughts of the powers and chose unerringly. It was very natural. Death came by many ways, yet was it all one after all,—a manifestation of the all-powerful and inscrutable.

But Hitchcock came of a later world-breed. His traditions were less concrete and without reverence, and he said, "Not so, Sipsu. You are young, and yet in the full joy of life. The witch doctor is a fool, and his choice is evil. This thing shall not be."

She smiled and answered, "Life is not kind, and for many reasons. First, it made of us twain the one white and the other red, which is bad. Then it crossed our trails, and now it parts them again; and we can do nothing. Once before, when the gods were angry, did your brothers come to the camp. They were three, big men and white, and they said the thing shall not be. But they died quickly, and the thing was."

Hitchcock nodded that he heard, half-turned, and lifted his voice. "Look here, you fellows! There's a lot of foolery going on over to the camp, and they're getting ready to murder Sipsu. What d'ye say?"

Wertz looked at Hawes, and Hawes looked back, but neither

103

spoke. Sigmund dropped his head, and petted the shepherd dog between his knees. He had brought Shep in with him from the outside, and thought a great deal of the animal. In fact, a certain girl, who was much in his thoughts, and whose picture in the little locket on his breast often inspired him to sing, had given him the dog and her blessing when they kissed good-by and he started on his Northland quest.

"What d'ye say?" Hitchcock repeated.

"Mebbe it's not so serious," Hawes answered with deliberation. "Most likely it's only a girl's story."

"That isn't the point!" Hitchcock felt a hot flush of anger sweep over him at their evident reluctance. "The question is, if it is so, are we going to stand it? What are we going to do?"

"I don't see any call to interfere," spoke up Wertz. "If it is so, it is so, and that's all there is about it. It's a way these people have of doing. It's their religion, and it's no concern of ours. Our concern is to get the dust and then get out of this God-forsaken land. T isn't fit for naught else but beasts? And what are these black devils but beasts? Besides, it'd be damn poor policy."

"That's what I say," chimed in Hawes. "Here we are, four of us, three hundred miles from the Yukon or a white face. And what can we do against half-a-hundred Indians? If we quarrel with them, we have to vamose; if we fight, we are wiped out. Further, we've struck pay, and, by God! I, for one, am going to stick by it!"

"Ditto here," supplemented Wertz.

Hitchcock turned impatiently to Sigmund, who was softly singing,—

"In a year, in a year, when the grapes are ripe,
    I shall stay no more away."

"Well, it's this way, Hitchcock," he finally said, "I'm in the same boat with the rest. If three-score bucks have made up their mind to kill the girl, why, we can't help it. One rush, and we'd be wiped off the landscape. And what good'd that be? They'd still have the girl. There's no use in going against the customs of a people except you're in force."

"But we are in force!" Hitchcock broke in. "Four whites are a match for a hundred times as many reds. And think of the girl!"

Sigmund stroked the dog meditatively. "But I do think of the girl. And her eyes are blue like summer skies, and laughing like summer seas, and her hair is yellow, like mine, and braided in ropes the size of a big man's arms. She's waiting for me, out there, in a better land. And she's waited long, and now my pile's in sight I'm not going to throw it away."

"And shamed I would be to look into the girl's blue eyes and remember the black ones of the girl whose blood was on my hands," Hitchcock sneered; for he was born to honor and championship, and to do the thing for the thing's sake, nor stop to weigh or measure.

Sigmund shook his head. "You can't make me mad, Hitchcock, nor do mad things because of your madness. It's a cold business proposition and a question of facts. I didn't come to this country for my health, and, further, it's impossible for us to raise a hand. If it is so, it is too bad for the girl, that's all. It's a way of her people, and it just happens we're on the spot this one time. They've done the same for a thousand-thousand years, and they're going to do it now, and they'll go on doing it for all time to come. Besides, they're not our kind. Nor's the girl. No, I take my stand with Wertz and Hawes, and—"

But the dogs snarled and drew in, and he broke off, listening to the crunch-crunch of many snowshoes. Indian after Indian stalked into the firelight, tall and grim, fur-clad and silent, their shadows dancing grotesquely on the snow. One,

105

the witch doctor, spoke gutturally to Sipsu. His face was daubed with savage paint blotches, and over his shoulders was drawn a wolfskin, the gleaming teeth and cruel snout surmounting his head. No other word was spoken. The prospectors held the peace. Sipsu arose and slipped into her snowshoes.

"Good-by, O my man," she said to Hitchcock. But the man who had sat beside her on the sled gave no sign, nor lifted his head as they filed away into the white forest.

Unlike many men, his faculty of adaptation, while large, had never suggested the expediency of an alliance with the women of the Northland. His broad cosmopolitanism had never impelled toward covenanting in marriage with the daughters of the soil. If it had, his philosophy of life would not have stood between. But it simply had not. Sipsu? He had pleasured in camp-fire chats with her, not as a man who knew himself to be man and she woman, but as a man might with a child, and as a man of his make certainly would if for no other reason than to vary the tedium of a bleak existence. That was all. But there was a certain chivalric thrill of warm blood in him, despite his Yankee ancestry and New England upbringing, and he was so made that the commercial aspect of life often seemed meaningless and bore contradiction to his deeper impulses.

So he sat silent, with head bowed forward, an organic force, greater than himself, as great as his race, at work within him. Wertz and Hawes looked askance at him from time to time, a faint but perceptible trepidation in their manner. Sigmund also felt this. Hitchcock was strong, and his strength had been impressed upon them in the course of many an event in their precarious life. So they stood in a certain definite awe and curiosity as to what his conduct would be when he moved to action.

But his silence was long, and the fire nigh out, when Wertz stretched his arms and yawned, and thought he'd go to bed. Then Hitchcock stood up his full height.

"May God damn your souls to the deepest hells, you chicken-hearted cowards! I'm done with you!" He said it calmly enough, but his strength spoke in every syllable, and every intonation was advertisement of intention. "Come on," he continued, "whack up, and in whatever way suits you best. I own a quarter-interest in the claims; our contracts show that. There're twenty-five or thirty ounces in the sack from the test pans. Fetch out the scales. We'll divide that now. And you, Sigmund, measure me my quarter-share of the grub and set it apart. Four of the dogs are mine, and I want four more. I'll trade you my share in the camp outfit and mining-gear for the dogs. And I'll throw in my six or seven ounces and the spare 45-90 with the ammunition. What d'ye say?"

The three men drew apart and conferred. When they returned, Sigmund acted as spokesman. "We'll whack up fair with you, Hitchcock. In everything you'll get your quarter-share, neither more nor less; and you can take it or leave it. But we want the dogs as bad as you do, so you get four, and that's all. If you don't want to take your share of the outfit and gear, why, that's your lookout. If you want it, you can have it; if you don't, leave it."

"The letter of the law," Hitchcock sneered. "But go ahead. I'm willing. And hurry up. I can't get out of this camp and away from its vermin any too quick."

The division was effected without further comment. He lashed his meagre belongings upon one of the sleds, rounded in his four dogs, and harnessed up. His portion of outfit and gear he did not touch, though he threw onto the sled half a dozen dog harnesses, and challenged them with his eyes to interfere. But they shrugged their shoulders and watched him disappear in the forest.

* * * * *

A man crawled upon his belly through the snow. On every hand loomed the moose-hide lodges of the camp. Here and there a miserable dog howled or snarled abuse upon his neighbor. Once, one of them approached the creeping man, but the man became motionless. The dog came closer and sniffed, and came yet closer, till its nose touched the strange object which had not been there when darkness fell. Then Hitchcock, for it was Hitchcock, upreared suddenly, shooting an unmittened hand out to the brute's shaggy throat. And the dog knew its death in that clutch, and when the man moved on, was left broken-necked under the stars. In this manner Hitchcock made the chief's lodge. For long he lay in the snow without, listening to the voices of the occupants and striving to locate Sipsu. Evidently there were many in the tent, and from the sounds they were in high excitement. At last he heard the girl's voice, and crawled around so that only the moose-hide divided them. Then burrowing in the snow, he slowly wormed his head and shoulders underneath. When the warm inner air smote his face, he stopped and waited, his legs and the greater part of his body still on the outside. He could see nothing, nor did he dare lift his head. On one side of him was a skin bale. He could smell it, though he carefully felt to be certain. On the other side his face barely touched a furry garment which he knew clothed a body. This must be Sipsu. Though he wished she would speak again, he resolved to risk it.

He could hear the chief and the witch doctor talking high, and in a far corner some hungry child whimpering to sleep. Squirming over on his side, he carefully raised his head, still just touching the furry garment. He listened to the breathing. It was a woman's breathing; he would chance it.

He pressed against her side softly but firmly, and felt her start at the contact. Again he waited, till a questioning hand slipped down upon his head and paused among the curls. The next instant the hand turned his face gently upward, and he was gazing into Sipsu's eyes.

She was quite collected. Changing her position casually, she threw an elbow well over on the skin bale, rested her body upon it, and arranged her *parka*. In this way he was completely concealed. Then, and still most casually, she reclined across him, so that he could breathe between her arm and breast, and when she lowered her head her ear pressed lightly against his lips.

"When the time suits, go thou," he whispered, "out of the lodge and across the snow, down the wind to the bunch of jackpine in the curve of the creek. There wilt thou find my dogs and my sled, packed for the trail. This night we go down to the Yukon; and since we go fast, lay thou hands upon what dogs come nigh thee, by the scruff of the neck, and drag them to the sled in the curve of the creek."

Sipsu shook her head in dissent; but her eyes glistened with gladness, and she was proud that this man had shown toward her such favor. But she, like the women of all her race, was born to obey the will masculine, and when Hitchcock repeated "Go!" he did it with authority, and though she made no answer he knew that his will was law.

"And never mind harness for the dogs," he added, preparing to go. "I shall wait. But waste no time. The day chaseth the night alway, nor does it linger for man's pleasure."

Half an hour later, stamping his feet and swinging his arms by the sled, he saw her coming, a surly dog in either hand. At the approach of these his own animals waxed truculent, and he favored them with the butt of his whip till they quieted. He had approached the camp up the wind, and sound was the thing to be most feared in making his presence known.

"Put them into the sled," he ordered when she had got the harness on the two dogs. "I want my leaders to the fore."

But when she had done this, the displaced animals pitched upon the aliens. Though Hitchcock plunged among them with clubbed rifle, a riot of sound went up and across the sleeping camp.

"Now we shall have dogs, and in plenty," he remarked grimly, slipping an axe from the sled lashings. "Do thou harness whichever I fling thee, and betweenwhiles protect the team."

He stepped a space in advance and waited between two pines. The dogs of the camp were disturbing the night with their jangle, and he watched for their coming. A dark spot, growing rapidly, took form upon the dim white expanse of snow. It was a forerunner of the pack, leaping cleanly, and, after the wolf fashion, singing direction to its brothers. Hitchcock stood in the shadow. As it sprang past, he reached out, gripped its forelegs in mid-career, and sent it whirling earthward. Then he struck it a well-judged blow beneath the ear, and flung it to Sipsu. And while she clapped on the harness, he, with his axe, held the passage between the trees, till a shaggy flood of white teeth and glistening eyes surged and crested just beyond reach. Sipsu worked rapidly. When she had finished, he leaped forward, seized and stunned a second, and flung it to her. This he repeated thrice again, and when the sled team stood snarling in a string of ten, he called, "Enough!"

But at this instant a young buck, the forerunner of the tribe, and swift of limb, wading through the dogs and cuffing right and left, attempted the passage. The butt of Hitchcock's rifle drove him to his knees, whence he toppled over sideways. The witch doctor, running lustily, saw the blow fall.

Hitchcock called to Sipsu to pull out. At her shrill "Chook!" the maddened brutes shot straight ahead, and the sled, bounding mightily, just missed unseating her. The powers were evidently angry with the witch doctor, for at this moment they plunged him upon the trail. The lead-dog fouled his snowshoes and tripped him up, and the nine succeeding dogs trod him under foot and the sled bumped over him. But he was quick to his feet, and the night might have turned out differently had not Sipsu struck backward with the long dog-whip and smitten him a blinding blow across the eyes. Hitchcock, hurrying to overtake her, collided against him as he swayed with pain in the middle of

110

the trail. Thus it was, when this primitive theologian got back to the chief's lodge, that his wisdom had been increased in so far as concerns the efficacy of the white man's fist. So, when he orated then and there in the council, he was wroth against all white men.

* * * * *

"Tumble out, you loafers! Tumble out! Grub'll be ready before you get into your footgear!"

Dave Wertz threw off the bearskin, sat up, and yawned.

Hawes stretched, discovered a lame muscle in his arm, and rubbed it sleepily. "Wonder where Hitchcock bunked last night?" he queried, reaching for his moccasins. They were stiff, and he walked gingerly in his socks to the fire to thaw them out. "It's a blessing he's gone," he added, "though he was a mighty good worker."

"Yep. Too masterful. That was his trouble. Too bad for Sipsu. Think he cared for her much?"

"Don't think so. Just principle. That's all. He thought it wasn't right—and, of course, it wasn't,—but that was no reason for us to interfere and get hustled over the divide before our time."

"Principle is principle, and it's good in its place, but it's best left to home when you go to Alaska. Eh?" Wertz had joined his mate, and both were working pliability into their frozen moccasins. "Think we ought to have taken a hand?"

Sigmund shook his head. He was very busy. A scud of chocolate-colored foam was rising in the coffee-pot, and the bacon needed turning. Also, he was thinking about the girl with laughing eyes like summer seas, and he was humming softly.

His mates chuckled to each other and ceased talking.

111

Though it was past seven, daybreak was still three hours distant. The aurora borealis had passed out of the sky, and the camp was an oasis of light in the midst of deep darkness. And in this light the forms of the three men were sharply defined. Emboldened by the silence, Sigmund raised his voice and opened the last stanza of the old song:-

"In a year, in a year, when the grapes are ripe—"

Then the night was split with a rattling volley of rifle-shots. Hawes sighed, made an effort to straighten himself, and collapsed. Wertz went over on an elbow with drooping head. He choked a little, and a dark stream flowed from his mouth. And Sigmund, the Golden-Haired, his throat a-gurgle with the song, threw up his arms and pitched across the fire.

* * * * *

The witch doctor's eyes were well blackened, and his temper none of the best; for he quarrelled with the chief over the possession of Wertz's rifle, and took more than his share of the part-sack of beans. Also he appropriated the bearskin, and caused grumbling among the tribesmen. And finally, he tried to kill Sigmund's dog, which the girl had given him, but the dog ran away, while he fell into the shaft and dislocated his shoulder on the bucket. When the camp was well looted they went back to their own lodges, and there was a great rejoicing among the women. Further, a band of moose strayed over the south divide and fell before the hunters, so the witch doctor attained yet greater honor, and the people whispered among themselves that he spoke in council with the gods.

But later, when all were gone, the shepherd dog crept back to the deserted camp, and all the night long and a day it wailed the dead. After that it disappeared, though the years were not many before the Indian hunters noted a change in the breed of timber wolves, and there were dashes of bright color and variegated markings such as no wolf bore before.

112

A DAUGHTER OF THE AURORA

"You—what you call—lazy mans, you lazy mans would desire me to haf for wife. It is not good. Nevaire, no, nevaire, will lazy mans my hoosband be."

Thus Joy Molineau spoke her mind to Jack Harrington, even as she had spoken it, but more tritely and in his own tongue, to Louis Savoy the previous night.

"Listen, Joy—"

"No, no; why moos' I listen to lazy mans? It is vaire bad, you hang rount, make visitation to my cabin, and do nothing. How you get grub for the famine? Why haf not you the dust? Odder mans haf plentee."

"But I work hard, Joy. Never a day am I not on trail or up creek. Even now have I just come off. My dogs are yet tired. Other men have luck and find plenty of gold; but I—I have no luck."

"Ah! But when this mans with the wife which is Indian, this mans McCormack, when him discovaire the Klondike, you go not. Odder mans go; odder mans now rich."

"You know I was prospecting over on the head-reaches of the Tanana," Harrington protested, "and knew nothing of the Eldorado or Bonanza until it was too late."

"That is deeferent; only you are—what you call way off."

"What?"

113

"Way off. In the—yes—in the dark. It is nevaire too late. One vaire rich mine is there, on the creek which is Eldorado. The mans drive the stake and him go 'way. No odddr mans know what of him become. The mans, him which drive the stake, is nevaire no more. Sixty days no mans on that claim file the papaire. Then odder mans, plentee odder mans— what you call—jump that claim. Then they race, O so queek, like the wind, to file the papaire. Him be vaire rich. Him get grub for famine."

Harrington hid the major portion of his interest.

"When's the time up?" he asked. "What claim is it?"

"So I speak Louis Savoy last night," she continued, ignoring him. "Him I think the winnaire."

"Hang Louis Savoy!"

"So Louis Savoy speak in my cabin last night. Him say, 'Joy, I am strong mans. I haf good dogs. I haf long wind. I will be winnaire. Then you will haf me for hoosband?' And I say to him, I say—"

"What'd you say?"

"I say, 'If Louis Savoy is winnaire, then will he haf me for wife.'"

"And if he don't win?"

"Then Louis Savoy, him will not be—what you call—the father of my children."

"And if I win?"

"You winnaire? Ha! ha! Nevaire!"

Exasperating as it was, Joy Molineau's laughter was pretty to

114

hear. Harrington did not mind it. He had long since been broken in. Besides, he was no exception. She had forced all her lovers to suffer in kind. And very enticing she was just then, her lips parted, her color heightened by the sharp kiss of the frost, her eyes vibrant with the lure which is the greatest of all lures and which may be seen nowhere save in woman's eyes. Her sled-dogs clustered about her in hirsute masses, and the leader, Wolf Fang, laid his long snout softly in her lap.

"If I do win?" Harrington pressed.

She looked from dog to lover and back again.

"What you say, Wolf Fang? If him strong mans and file the papaire, shall we his wife become? Eh? What you say?"

Wolf Fang picked up his ears and growled at Harrington.

"It is vaire cold," she suddenly added with feminine irrelevance, rising to her feet and straightening out the team.

Her lover looked on stolidly. She had kept him guessing from the first time they met, and patience had been joined unto his virtues.

"Hi! Wolf Fang!" she cried, springing upon the sled as it leaped into sudden motion. "Ai! Ya! Mush-on!"

From the corner of his eye Harrington watched her swinging down the trail to Forty Mile. Where the road forked and crossed the river to Fort Cudahy, she halted the dogs and turned about.

"O Mistaire Lazy Mans!" she called back. "Wolf Fang, him say yes—if you winnaire!"

But somehow, as such things will, it leaked out, and all Forty Mile, which had hitherto speculated on Joy Molineau's choice between her two latest lovers, now hazarded bets and

115

guesses as to which would win in the forthcoming race. The camp divided itself into two factions, and every effort was put forth in order that their respective favorites might be the first in at the finish. There was a scramble for the best dogs the country could afford, for dogs, and good ones, were essential, above all, to success. And it meant much to the victor. Besides the possession of a wife, the like of which had yet to be created, it stood for a mine worth a million at least.

That fall, when news came down of McCormack's discovery on Bonanza, all the Lower Country, Circle City and Forty Mile included, had stampeded up the Yukon,—at least all save those who, like Jack Harrington and Louis Savoy, were away prospecting in the west. Moose pastures and creeks were staked indiscriminately and promiscuously; and incidentally, one of the unlikeliest of creeks, Eldorado. Olaf Nelson laid claim to five hundred of its linear feet, duly posted his notice, and as duly disappeared. At that time the nearest recording office was in the police barracks at Fort Cudahy, just across the river from Forty Mile; but when it became bruited abroad that Eldorado Creek was a treasure-house, it was quickly discovered that Olaf Nelson had failed to make the down-Yukon trip to file upon his property. Men cast hungry eyes upon the ownerless claim, where they knew a thousand-thousand dollars waited but shovel and sluice-box. Yet they dared not touch it; for there was a law which permitted sixty days to lapse between the staking and the filing, during which time a claim was immune. The whole country knew of Olaf Nelson's disappearance, and scores of men made preparation for the jumping and for the consequent race to Fort Cudahy.

But competition at Forty Mile was limited. With the camp devoting its energies to the equipping either of Jack Harrington or Louis Savoy, no man was unwise enough to enter the contest single-handed. It was a stretch of a hundred miles to the Recorder's office, and it was planned that the two favorites should have four relays of dogs stationed along the trail. Naturally, the last relay was to be the crucial one, and for these twenty-five miles their respective partisans strove to obtain the strongest possible animals. So bitter did the factions wax, and so high did they bid, that dogs brought stiffer prices than ever before in the annals of the country. And, as it chanced, this scramble for dogs turned the public eye still more searchingly upon Joy Molineau. Not only was she the cause of it all, but she possessed the finest sled-dog from Chilkoot to Bering Sea. As wheel or leader, Wolf Fang had no equal. The man whose sled he led down the last stretch was bound to win. There could be no doubt of it. But the community had an innate sense of the fitness of things, and not once was Joy vexed by overtures for his use. And the factions drew consolation from the fact that if one man did not profit by him, neither should the other.

However, since man, in the individual or in the aggregate, has been so fashioned that he goes through life blissfully obtuse to the deeper subtleties of his womankind, so the men of Forty Mile failed to divine the inner deviltry of Joy Molineau. They confessed, afterward, that they had failed to appreciate this dark-eyed daughter of the aurora, whose father had traded furs in the country before ever they dreamed of invading it, and who had herself first opened eyes on the scintillant northern lights. Nay, accident of birth had not rendered her less the woman, nor had it limited her woman's understanding of men. They knew she played with them, but they did not know the wisdom of her play, its deepness and its deftness. They failed to see more than the exposed card, so that to the very last Forty Mile was in a state of pleasant obfuscation, and it was not until she cast her final trump that it came to reckon up the score.

Early in the week the camp turned out to start Jack Harrington and Louis Savoy on their way. They had taken a shrewd margin of time, for it was their wish to arrive at Olaf Nelson's claim some days previous to the expiration of its immunity, that they might rest themselves, and their dogs be fresh for the first relay. On the way up they found the men of Dawson already stationing spare dog teams along the trail,

117

and it was manifest that little expense had been spared in view of the millions at stake.

A couple of days after the departure of their champions, Forty Mile began sending up their relays,—first to the seventy-five station, then to the fifty, and last to the twenty-five. The teams for the last stretch were magnificent, and so equally matched that the camp discussed their relative merits for a full hour at fifty below, before they were permitted to pull out. At the last moment Joy Molineau dashed in among them on her sled. She drew Lon McFane, who had charge of Harrington's team, to one side, and hardly had the first words left her lips when it was noticed that his lower jaw dropped with a celerity and emphasis suggestive of great things. He unhitched Wolf Fang from her sled, put him at the head of Harrington's team, and mushed the string of animals into the Yukon trail.

"Poor Louis Savoy!" men said; but Joy Molineau flashed her black eyes defiantly and drove back to her father's cabin.

* * * * *

Midnight drew near on Olaf Nelson's claim. A few hundred fur-clad men had preferred sixty below and the jumping, to the inducements of warm cabins and comfortable bunks. Several score of them had their notices prepared for posting and their dogs at hand. A bunch of Captain Constantine's mounted police had been ordered on duty that fair play might rule. The command had gone forth that no man should place a stake till the last second of the day had ticked itself into the past. In the northland such commands are equal to Jehovah's in the matter of potency; the dum-dum as rapid and effective as the thunderbolt. It was clear and cold. The aurora borealis painted palpitating color revels on the sky. Rosy waves of cold brilliancy swept across the zenith, while great coruscating bars of greenish white blotted out the stars, or a Titan's hand reared mighty arches above the Pole. And at this mighty display the wolf-dogs howled as had their ancestors of old time.

A bearskin-coated policeman stepped prominently to the fore, watch in hand. Men hurried among the dogs, rousing them to their feet, untangling their traces, straightening them out. The entries came to the mark, firmly gripping stakes and notices. They had gone over the boundaries of the claim so often that they could now have done it blindfolded. The policeman raised his hand. Casting off their superfluous furs and blankets, and with a final cinching of belts, they came to attention.

"Time!"

Sixty pairs of hands unmitted; as many pairs of moccasins gripped hard upon the snow.

"Go!"

They shot across the wide expanse, round the four sides, sticking notices at every corner, and down the middle where the two centre stakes were to be planted. Then they sprang for the sleds on the frozen bed of the creek. An anarchy of sound and motion broke out. Sled collided with sled, and dog-team fastened upon dog-team with bristling manes and screaming fangs. The narrow creek was glutted with the struggling mass. Lashes and butts of dog-whips were distributed impartially among men and brutes. And to make it of greater moment, each participant had a bunch of comrades intent on breaking him out of jam. But one by one, and by sheer strength, the sleds crept out and shot from sight in the darkness of the overhanging banks.

Jack Harrington had anticipated this crush and waited by his sled until it untangled. Louis Savoy, aware of his rival's greater wisdom in the matter of dog-driving, had followed his lead and also waited. The rout had passed beyond earshot when they took the trail, and it was not till they had travelled the ten miles or so down to Bonanza that they came upon it, speeding along in single file, but well bunched. There was little noise, and less chance of one passing another at that stage. The sleds, from runner to runner, measured sixteen inches, the trail eighteen; but the trail, packed down fully a foot by the traffic, was like a gutter. On either side spread the blanket of soft snow crystals. If a man turned into this in an endeavor to pass, his dogs would wallow perforce to their bellies and slow down to a snail's pace. So the men lay close to their leaping sleds and waited. No alteration in position occurred down the fifteen miles of Bonanza and Klondike to Dawson, where the Yukon was encountered. Here the first relays waited. But here, intent to kill their first teams, if necessary, Harrington and Savoy had had their fresh teams placed a couple of miles beyond those of the others. In the confusion of changing sleds they passed full half the bunch. Perhaps thirty men were still leading them when they shot on to the broad breast of the Yukon. Here was the tug. When the river froze in the fall, a mile of open water had been left between two mighty jams. This had but recently crusted, the current being swift, and now it was as level, hard, and slippery as a dance floor. The instant they struck this glare ice Harrington came to his knees, holding precariously on with one hand, his whip singing fiercely among his dogs and fearsome abjurations hurtling about their ears. The teams spread out on the smooth surface, each straining to the uttermost. But few men in the North could lift their dogs as did Jack Harrington. At once he began to pull ahead, and Louis Savoy, taking the pace, hung on desperately, his leaders running even with the tail of his rival's sled.

Midway on the glassy stretch their relays shot out from the bank. But Harrington did not slacken. Watching his chance when the new sled swung in close, he leaped across, shouting as he did so and jumping up the pace of his fresh dogs. The other driver fell off somehow. Savoy did likewise with his relay, and the abandoned teams, swerving to right and left, collided with the others and piled the ice with confusion. Harrington cut out the pace; Savoy hung on. As they neared the end of the glare ice, they swept abreast of the leading sled. When they shot into the narrow trail between the soft snowbanks, they led the race; and Dawson, watching by the light of the aurora, swore that it was neatly done.

When the frost grows lusty at sixty below, men cannot long remain without fire or excessive exercise, and live. So Harrington and Savoy now fell to the ancient custom of "ride and run." Leaping from their sleds, tow-thongs in hand, they ran behind till the blood resumed its wonted channels and expelled the frost, then back to the sleds till the heat again ebbed away. Thus, riding and running, they covered the second and third relays. Several times, on smooth ice, Savoy spurted his dogs, and as often failed to gain past. Strung along for five miles in the rear, the remainder of the race strove to overtake them, but vainly, for to Louis Savoy alone was the glory given of keeping Jack Harrington's killing pace.

As they swung into the seventy-five-mile station, Lon McFane dashed alongside; Wolf Fang in the lead caught Harrington's eye, and he knew that the race was his. No team in the North could pass him on those last twenty-five miles. And when Savoy saw Wolf Fang heading his rival's team, he knew that he was out of the running, and he cursed softly to himself, in the way woman is most frequently cursed. But he still clung to the other's smoking trail, gambling on chance to the last. And as they churned along, the day breaking in the southeast, they marvelled in joy and sorrow at that which Joy Molineau had done.

* * * * *

Forty Mile had early crawled out of its sleeping furs and congregated near the edge of the trail. From this point it could view the up-Yukon course to its first bend several miles away. Here it could also see across the river to the finish at Fort Cudahy, where the Gold Recorder nervously awaited. Joy Molineau had taken her position several rods back from the trail, and under the circumstances, the rest of Forty Mile forbore interposing itself. So the space was clear between her and the slender line of the course. Fires had been built, and around these men wagered dust and dogs, the long odds on Wolf Fang.

"Here they come!" shrilled an Indian boy from the top of a pine.

Up the Yukon a black speck appeared against the snow, closely followed by a second. As these grew larger, more black specks manifested themselves, but at a goodly distance to the rear. Gradually they resolved themselves into dogs and sleds, and men lying flat upon them. "Wolf Fang leads," a lieutenant of police whispered to Joy. She smiled her interest back.

"Ten to one on Harrington!" cried a Birch Creek King, dragging out his sack.

"The Queen, her pay you not mooch?" queried Joy.

The lieutenant shook his head.

"You have some dust, ah, how mooch?" she continued.

He exposed his sack. She gauged it with a rapid eye.

"Mebbe—say—two hundred, eh? Good. Now I give—what you call—the tip. Covaire the bet." Joy smiled inscrutably. The lieutenant pondered. He glanced up the trail. The two men had risen to their knees and were lashing their dogs furiously, Harrington in the lead.

"Ten to one on Harrington!" bawled the Birch Creek King, flourishing his sack in the lieutenant's face.

"Covaire the bet," Joy prompted.

He obeyed, shrugging his shoulders in token that he yielded, not to the dictate of his reason, but to her charm. Joy nodded to reassure him.

122

All noise ceased. Men paused in the placing of bets.

Yawing and reeling and plunging, like luggers before the wind, the sleds swept wildly upon them. Though he still kept his leader up to the tail of Harrington's sled, Louis Savoy's face was without hope. Harrington's mouth was set. He looked neither to the right nor to the left. His dogs were leaping in perfect rhythm, firm-footed, close to the trail, and Wolf Fang, head low and unseeing, whining softly, was leading his comrades magnificently.

Forty Mile stood breathless. Not a sound, save the roar of the runners and the voice of the whips.

Then the clear voice of Joy Molineau rose on the air. "Ai! Ya! Wolf Fang! Wolf Fang!"

Wolf Fang heard. He left the trail sharply, heading directly for his mistress. The team dashed after him, and the sled poised an instant on a single runner, then shot Harrington into the snow. Savoy was by like a flash. Harrington pulled to his feet and watched him skimming across the river to the Gold Recorder's. He could not help hearing what was said.

"Ah, him do vaire well," Joy Molineau was explaining to the lieutenant. "Him—what you call—set the pace. Yes, him set the pace vaire well."

AT THE RAINBOW'S END

It was for two reasons that Montana Kid discarded his "chaps" and Mexican spurs, and shook the dust of the Idaho ranges from his feet. In the first place, the encroachments of a steady, sober, and sternly moral civilization had destroyed the primeval status of the western cattle ranges, and refined society turned the cold eye of disfavor upon him and his ilk. In the second place, in one of its cyclopean moments the race had arisen and shoved back its frontier several thousand miles. Thus, with unconscious foresight, did mature society make room for its adolescent members. True, the new territory was mostly barren; but its several hundred thousand square miles of frigidity at least gave breathing space to those who else would have suffocated at home.

Montana Kid was such a one. Heading for the sea-coast, with a haste several sheriff's posses might possibly have explained, and with more nerve than coin of the realm, he succeeded in shipping from a Puget Sound port, and managed to survive the contingent miseries of steerage sea-sickness and steerage grub. He was rather sallow and drawn, but still his own indomitable self, when he landed on the Dyea beach one day in the spring of the year. Between the cost of dogs, grub, and outfits, and the customs exactions of the two clashing governments, it speedily penetrated to his understanding that the Northland was anything save a poor man's Mecca. So he cast about him in search of quick harvests. Between the beach and the passes were scattered many thousands of passionate pilgrims. These pilgrims Montana Kid proceeded to farm. At first he dealt faro in a pine-board gambling shack; but disagreeable necessity forced him to drop a sudden period into a man's life, and to move on up trail. Then he effected a corner in horseshoe nails, and they circulated at par with legal tender, four to the dollar, till an unexpected consignment of a hundred barrels or so broke the market and forced him to disgorge his stock at a loss. After that he located at Sheep Camp, organized the professional packers, and jumped the freight ten cents a pound in a single day. In token of their gratitude, the packers patronized his faro and roulette layouts and were mulcted cheerfully of their earnings. But his commercialism was of too lusty a growth to be long endured; so they rushed him one night, burned his shanty, divided the bank, and headed him up the trail with empty pockets.

Ill-luck was his running mate. He engaged with responsible parties to run whisky across the line by way of precarious and unknown trails, lost his Indian guides, and had the very first outfit confiscated by the Mounted Police. Numerous other misfortunes tended to make him bitter of heart and wanton of action, and he celebrated his arrival at Lake Bennett by terrorizing the camp for twenty straight hours. Then a miners' meeting took him in hand, and commanded him to make himself scarce. He had a wholesome respect for such assemblages, and he obeyed in such haste that he inadvertently removed himself at the tail-end of another man's dog team. This was equivalent to horse-stealing in a more mellow clime, so he hit only the high places across Bennett and down Tagish, and made his first camp a full hundred miles to the north.

Now it happened that the break of spring was at hand, and many of the principal citizens of Dawson were travelling south on the last ice. These he met and talked with, noted their names and possessions, and passed on. He had a good memory, also a fair imagination; nor was veracity one of his virtues.

II

Dawson, always eager for news, beheld Montana Kid's sled

heading down the Yukon, and went out on the ice to meet him. No, he hadn't any newspapers; didn't know whether Durrant was hanged yet, nor who had won the Thanksgiving game; hadn't heard whether the United States and Spain had gone to fighting; didn't know who Dreyfus was; but O'Brien? Hadn't they heard? O'Brien, why, he was drowned in the White Horse; Sitka Charley the only one of the party who escaped. Joe Ladue? Both legs frozen and amputated at the Five Fingers. And Jack Dalton? Blown up on the "Sea Lion" with all hands. And Bettles? Wrecked on the "Carthagina," in Seymour Narrows,—twenty survivors out of three hundred. And Swiftwater Bill? Gone through the rotten ice of Lake LeBarge with six female members of the opera troupe he was convoying. Governor Walsh? Lost with all hands and eight sleds on the Thirty Mile. Devereaux? Who was Devereaux? Oh, the courier! Shot by Indians on Lake Marsh.

So it went. The word was passed along. Men shouldered in to ask after friends and partners, and in turn were shouldered out, too stunned for blasphemy. By the time Montana Kid gained the bank he was surrounded by several hundred fur-clad miners. When he passed the Barracks he was the centre of a procession. At the Opera House he was the nucleus of an excited mob, each member struggling for a chance to ask after some absent comrade. On every side he was being invited to drink. Never before had the Klondike thus opened its arms to a che-cha-qua. All Dawson was humming. Such a series of catastrophes had never occurred in its history. Every man of note who had gone south in the spring had been wiped out. The cabins vomited forth their occupants. Wild-eyed men hurried down from the creeks and gulches to seek out this man who had told a tale of such disaster. The Russian half-breed wife of Bettles sought the fireplace, inconsolable, and rocked back and forth, and ever and anon flung white wood-ashes upon her raven hair. The flag at the Barracks flopped dismally at half-mast. Dawson mourned its dead.

Why Montana Kid did this thing no man may know. Nor

126

beyond the fact that the truth was not in him, can explanation be hazarded. But for five whole days he plunged the land in wailing and sorrow, and for five whole days he was the only man in the Klondike. The country gave him its best of bed and board. The saloons granted him the freedom of their bars. Men sought him continuously. The high officials bowed down to him for further information, and he was feasted at the Barracks by Constantine and his brother officers. And then, one day, Devereaux, the government courier, halted his tired dogs before the gold commissioner's office. Dead? Who said so? Give him a moose steak and he'd show them how dead he was. Why, Governor Walsh was in camp on the Little Salmon, and O'Brien coming in on the first water. Dead? Give him a moose steak and he'd show them.

And forthwith Dawson hummed. The Barracks' flag rose to the masthead, and Bettles' wife washed herself and put on clean raiment. The community subtly signified its desire that Montana Kid obliterate himself from the landscape. And Montana Kid obliterated; as usual, at the tail-end of some one else's dog team. Dawson rejoiced when he headed down the Yukon, and wished him godspeed to the ultimate destination of the case-hardened sinner. After that the owner of the dogs bestirred himself, made complaint to Constantine, and from him received the loan of a policeman.

III

With Circle City in prospect and the last ice crumbling under his runners, Montana Kid took advantage of the lengthening days and travelled his dogs late and early. Further, he had but little doubt that the owner of the dogs in question had taken his trail, and he wished to make American territory before the river broke. But by the afternoon of the third day it became evident that he had lost in his race with spring. The Yukon was growling and straining at its fetters. Long détours became necessary, for the trail had begun to fall through into the swift current beneath, while the ice, in constant unrest, was thundering apart in great gaping fissures. Through these and through countless airholes, the water began to sweep across the surface of the ice, and by the time he pulled into a woodchopper's cabin on the point of an island, the dogs were being rushed off their feet and were swimming more often than not. He was greeted sourly by the two residents, but he unharnessed and proceeded to cook up.

Donald and Davy were fair specimens of frontier inefficients. Canadian-born, city-bred Scots, in a foolish moment they had resigned their counting-house desks, drawn upon their savings, and gone Klondiking. And now they were feeling the rough edge of the country. Grubless, spiritless, with a lust for home in their hearts, they had been staked by the P. C. Company to cut wood for its steamers, with the promise at the end of a passage home. Disregarding the possibilities of the ice-run, they had fittingly demonstrated their inefficiency by their choice of the island on which they located. Montana Kid, though possessing little knowledge of the break-up of a great river, looked about him dubiously, and cast yearning glances at the distant bank where the towering bluffs promised immunity from all the ice of the Northland.

After feeding himself and dogs, he lighted his pipe and strolled out to get a better idea of the situation. The island, like all its river brethren, stood higher at the upper end, and it was here that Donald and Davy had built their cabin and piled many cords of wood. The far shore was a full mile away, while between the island and the near shore lay a back-channel perhaps a hundred yards across. At first sight of this, Montana Kid was tempted to take his dogs and escape to the mainland, but on closer inspection he discovered a rapid current flooding on top. Below, the river twisted sharply to the west, and in this turn its breast was studded by a maze of tiny islands.

"That's where she'll jam," he remarked to himself.

Half a dozen sleds, evidently bound up-stream to Dawson, were splashing through the chill water to the tail of the island. Travel on the river was passing from the precarious to the impossible, and it was nip and tuck with them till they gained the island and came up the path of the wood-choppers toward the cabin. One of them, snow-blind, towed helplessly at the rear of a sled. Husky young fellows they were, rough-garmented and trail-worn, yet Montana Kid had met the breed before and knew at once that it was not his kind.

"Hello! How's things up Dawson-way?" queried the foremost, passing his eye over Donald and Davy and settling it upon the Kid.

A first meeting in the wilderness is not characterized by formality. The talk quickly became general, and the news of the Upper and Lower Countries was swapped equitably back and forth. But the little the newcomers had was soon over with, for they had wintered at Minook, a thousand miles below, where nothing was doing. Montana Kid, however, was fresh from Salt Water, and they annexed him while they pitched camp, swamping him with questions concerning the outside, from which they had been cut off for a twelvemonth.

A shrieking split, suddenly lifting itself above the general uproar on the river, drew everybody to the bank. The surface water had increased in depth, and the ice, assailed from above and below, was struggling to tear itself from the grip of the shores. Fissures reverberated into life before their eyes, and the air was filled with multitudinous crackling, crisp and sharp, like the sound that goes up on a clear day from the firing line.

From up the river two men were racing a dog team toward them on an uncovered stretch of ice. But even as they looked, the pair struck the water and began to flounder through. Behind, where their feet had sped the moment before, the ice broke up and turned turtle. Through this opening the river rushed out upon them to their waists, burying the sled and swinging the dogs off at right angles in a drowning tangle. But the men stopped their flight to give the animals a fighting chance, and they groped hurriedly in the cold confusion, slashing at the detaining traces with their sheath-knives. Then they fought their way to the bank through swirling water and grinding ice, where, foremost in leaping to the rescue among the jarring fragments, was the Kid.

"Why, blime me, if it ain't Montana Kid!" exclaimed one of the men whom the Kid was just placing upon his feet at the top of the bank. He wore the scarlet tunic of the Mounted Police and jocularly raised his right hand in salute.

"Got a warrant for you, Kid," he continued, drawing a bedraggled paper from his breast pocket, "an' I 'ope as you'll come along peaceable."

Montana Kid looked at the chaotic river and shrugged his shoulders, and the policeman, following his glance, smiled.

"Where are the dogs?" his companion asked.

"Gentlemen," interrupted the policeman, "this 'ere mate o' mine is Jack Sutherland, owner of Twenty-Two Eldorado—"

"Not Sutherland of '92?" broke in the snow-blinded Minook man, groping feebly toward him.

"The same." Sutherland gripped his hand.

"And you?"

"Oh, I'm after your time, but I remember you in my freshman year,—you were doing P. G. work then. Boys," he called, turning half about, "this is Sutherland, Jack Sutherland, erstwhile full-back on the 'Varsity. Come up, you gold-chasers, and fall upon him! Sutherland, this is Greenwich,— played quarter two seasons back."

"Yes, I read of the game," Sutherland said, shaking hands.

130

"And I remember that big run of yours for the first touchdown."

Greenwich flushed darkly under his tanned skin and awkwardly made room for another.

"And here's Matthews,—Berkeley man. And we've got some Eastern cracks knocking about, too. Come up, you Princeton men! Come up! This is Sutherland, Jack Sutherland!"

Then they fell upon him heavily, carried him into camp, and supplied him with dry clothes and numerous mugs of black tea.

Donald and Davy, overlooked, had retired to their nightly game of crib. Montana Kid followed them with the policeman.

"Here, get into some dry togs," he said, pulling them from out his scanty kit. "Guess you'll have to bunk with me, too."

"Well, I say, you're a good 'un," the policeman remarked as he pulled on the other man's socks. "Sorry I've got to take you back to Dawson, but I only 'ope they won't be 'ard on you."

"Not so fast." The Kid smiled curiously. "We ain't under way yet. When I go I'm going down river, and I guess the chances are you'll go along."

"Not if I know myself—"

"Come on outside, and I'll show you, then. These damn fools," thrusting a thumb over his shoulder at the two Scots, "played smash when they located here. Fill your pipe, first—this is pretty good plug—and enjoy yourself while you can. You haven't many smokes before you."

The policeman went with him wonderingly, while Donald and

Davy dropped their cards and followed. The Minook men noticed Montana Kid pointing now up the river, now down, and came over.

"What's up?" Sutherland demanded.

"Nothing much." Nonchalance sat well upon the Kid. "Just a case of raising hell and putting a chunk under. See that bend down there? That's where she'll jam millions of tons of ice. Then she'll jam in the bends up above, millions of tons. Upper jam breaks first, lower jam holds, poufl" He dramatically swept the island with his hand. "Millions of tons," he added reflectively.

"And what of the woodpiles?" Davy questioned.

The Kid repeated his sweeping gestures and Davy wailed, "The labor of months! It canna be! Na, na, lad, it canna be. I doot not it's a jowk. Ay, say that it is," he appealed.

But when the Kid laughed harshly and turned on his heel, Davy flung himself upon the piles and began frantically to toss the cordwood back from the bank.

"Lend a hand, Donald!" he cried. "Can ye no lend a hand? 'T is the labor of months and the passage home!"

Donald caught him by the arm and shook him, but he tore free. "Did ye no hear, man? Millions of tons, and the island shall be sweepit clean."

"Straighten yersel' up, man," said Donald. "It's a bit fashed ye are."

But Davy fell upon the cordwood. Donald stalked back to the cabin, buckled on his money belt and Davy's, and went out to the point of the island where the ground was highest and where a huge pine towered above its fellows.

The men before the cabin heard the ringing of his axe and
132

smiled. Greenwich returned from across the island with the word that they were penned in. It was impossible to cross the back-channel. The blind Minook man began to sing, and the rest joined in with—

"Wonder if it's true?
Does it seem so to you?
Seems to me he's lying—
Oh, I wonder if it's true?"

"It's ay sinfu'," Davy moaned, lifting his head and watching them dance in the slanting rays of the sun. "And my guid wood a' going to waste."

"Oh, I wonder if it's true,"

was flaunted back.

The noise of the river ceased suddenly. A strange calm wrapped about them. The ice had ripped from the shores and was floating higher on the surface of the river, which was rising. Up it came, swift and silent, for twenty feet, till the huge cakes rubbed softly against the crest of the bank. The tail of the island, being lower, was overrun. Then, without effort, the white flood started down-stream. But the sound increased with the momentum, and soon the whole island was shaking and quivering with the shock of the grinding bergs. Under pressure, the mighty cakes, weighing hundreds of tons, were shot into the air like peas. The frigid anarchy increased its riot, and the men had to shout into one another's ears to be heard. Occasionally the racket from the back channel could be heard above the tumult. The island shuddered with the impact of an enormous cake which drove in squarely upon its point. It ripped a score of pines out by the roots, then swinging around and over, lifted its muddy base from the bottom of the river and bore down upon the cabin, slicing the bank and trees away like a gigantic knife. It seemed barely to graze the corner of the cabin, but the cribbed logs tilted up like matches, and the structure, like a toy house, fell backward in ruin.

"The labor of months! The labor of months, and the passage home!" Davy wailed, while Montana Kid and the policeman dragged him backward from the woodpiles.

"You'll 'ave plenty o' hoppertunity all in good time for yer passage 'ome," the policeman growled, clouting him alongside the head and sending him flying into safety.

Donald, from the top of the pine, saw the devastating berg sweep away the cordwood and disappear down-stream. As though satisfied with this damage, the ice-flood quickly dropped to its old level and began to slacken its pace. The noise likewise eased down, and the others could hear Donald shouting from his eyrie to look down-stream. As forecast, the jam had come among the islands in the bend, and the ice was piling up in a great barrier which stretched from shore to shore. The river came to a standstill, and the water finding no outlet began to rise. It rushed up till the island was awash, the men splashing around up to their knees, and the dogs swimming to the ruins of the cabin. At this stage it abruptly became stationary, with no perceptible rise or fall.

Montana Kid shook his head. "It's jammed above, and no more's coming down."

"And the gamble is, which jam will break first," Sutherland added.

"Exactly," the Kid affirmed. "If the upper jam breaks first, we haven't a chance. Nothing will stand before it."

The Minook men turned away in silence, but soon "Rumsky Ho" floated upon the quiet air, followed by "The Orange and the Black." Room was made in the circle for Montana Kid and the policeman, and they quickly caught the ringing rhythm of the choruses as they drifted on from song to song.

"Oh, Donald, will ye no lend a hand?" Davy sobbed at the foot of the tree into which his comrade had climbed. "Oh, Donald, man, will ye no lend a hand?" he sobbed again, his hands bleeding from vain attempts to scale the slippery trunk.

But Donald had fixed his gaze up river, and now his voice rang out, vibrant with fear:—

"God Almichty, here she comes!"

Standing knee-deep in the icy water, the Minook men, with Montana Kid and the policeman, gripped hands and raised their voices in the terrible, "Battle Hymn of the Republic." But the words were drowned in the advancing roar.

And to Donald was vouchsafed a sight such as no man may see and live. A great wall of white flung itself upon the island. Trees, dogs, men, were blotted out, as though the hand of God had wiped the face of nature clean. This much he saw, then swayed an instant longer in his lofty perch and hurtled far out into the frozen hell.

THE SCORN OF WOMEN

I

Once Freda and Mrs. Eppingwell clashed.

Now Freda was a Greek girl and a dancer. At least she purported to be Greek; but this was doubted by many, for her classic face had overmuch strength in it, and the tides of hell which rose in her eyes made at rare moments her ethnology the more dubious. To a few—men—this sight had been vouchsafed, and though long years may have passed, they have not forgotten, nor will they ever forget. She never talked of herself, so that it were well to let it go down that when in repose, expurgated, Greek she certainly was. Her furs were the most magnificent in all the country from Chilcoot to St. Michael's, and her name was common on the lips of men. But Mrs. Eppingwell was the wife of a captain; also a social constellation of the first magnitude, the path of her orbit marking the most select coterie in Dawson,—a coterie captioned by the profane as the "official clique." Sitka Charley had travelled trail with her once, when famine drew tight and a man's life was less than a cup of flour, and his judgment placed her above all women. Sitka Charley was an Indian; his criteria were primitive; but his word was flat, and his verdict a hall-mark in every camp under the circle.

These two women were man-conquering, man-subduing machines, each in her own way, and their ways were different. Mrs. Eppingwell ruled in her own house, and at the Barracks, where were younger sons galore, to say nothing of the chiefs of the police, the executive, and the judiciary. Freda ruled down in the town; but the men she ruled were the same who functioned socially at the Barracks or were fed tea and canned preserves at the hand of Mrs.

Eppingwell in her hillside cabin of rough-hewn logs. Each knew the other existed; but their lives were apart as the Poles, and while they must have heard stray bits of news and were curious, they were never known to ask a question. And there would have been no trouble had not a free lance in the shape of the model-woman come into the land on the first ice, with a spanking dog-team and a cosmopolitan reputation. Loraine Lisznayi—alliterative, dramatic, and Hungarian—precipitated the strife, and because of her Mrs. Eppingwell left her hillside and invaded Freda's domain, and Freda likewise went up from the town to spread confusion and embarrassment at the Governor's ball.

All of which may be ancient history so far as the Klondike is concerned, but very few, even in Dawson, know the inner truth of the matter; nor beyond those few are there any fit to measure the wife of the captain or the Greek dancer. And that all are now permitted to understand, let honor be accorded Sitka Charley. From his lips fell the main facts in the screed herewith presented. It ill befits that Freda herself should have waxed confidential to a mere scribbler of words, or that Mrs. Eppingwell made mention of the things which happened. They may have spoken, but it is unlikely.

II

Floyd Vanderlip was a strong man, apparently. Hard work and hard grub had no terrors for him, as his early history in the country attested. In danger he was a lion, and when he held in check half a thousand starving men, as he once did, it was remarked that no cooler eye ever took the glint of sunshine on a rifle-sight. He had but one weakness, and even that, rising from out his strength, was of a negative sort. His parts were strong, but they lacked co-ordination. Now it happened that while his centre of amativeness was pronounced, it had lain mute and passive during the years he lived on moose and salmon and chased glowing Eldorados over chill divides. But when he finally blazed the corner-post and centre-stakes on one of the richest Klondike claims, it began to quicken; and when he took his place in society, a full-fledged Bonanza King, it awoke and took charge of him. He suddenly recollected a girl in the States, and it came to him quite forcibly, not only that she might be waiting for him, but that a wife was a very pleasant acquisition for a man who lived some several degrees north of 53. So he wrote an appropriate note, enclosed a letter of credit generous enough to cover all expenses, including trousseau and chaperon, and addressed it to one Flossie. Flossie? One could imagine the rest. However, after that he built a comfortable cabin on his claim, bought another in Dawson, and broke the news to his friends.

And just here is where the lack of co-ordination came into play. The waiting was tedious, and having been long denied, the amative element could not brook further delay. Flossie was coming; but Loraine Lisznayi was here. And not only was Loraine Lisznayi here, but her cosmopolitan reputation was somewhat the worse for wear, and she was not exactly so young as when she posed in the studios of artist queens and received at her door the cards of cardinals and princes. Also, her finances were unhealthy. Having run the gamut in her time, she was now not averse to trying conclusions with a Bonanza King whose wealth was such that he could not guess it within six figures. Like a wise soldier casting about after years of service for a comfortable billet, she had come into the Northland to be married. So, one day, her eyes flashed up into Floyd Vanderlip's as he was buying table linen for Flossie in the P. C. Company's store, and the thing was settled out of hand.

When a man is free much may go unquestioned, which, should he be rash enough to cumber himself with domestic ties, society will instantly challenge. Thus it was with Floyd Vanderlip. Flossie was coming, and a low buzz went up when Loraine Lisznayi rode down the main street behind his wolf-dogs. She accompanied the lady reporter of the "Kansas City Star" when photographs were taken of his Bonanza properties, and watched the genesis of a six-column article. At that time they were dined royally in Flossie's cabin, on Flossie's table linen. Likewise there were comings and goings, and junketings, all perfectly proper, by the way, which caused the men to say sharp things and the women to be spiteful. Only Mrs. Eppingwell did not hear. The distant hum of wagging tongues rose faintly, but she was prone to believe good of people and to close her ears to evil; so she paid no heed.

Not so with Freda. She had no cause to love men, but, by some strange alchemy of her nature, her heart went out to women,—to women whom she had less cause to love. And her heart went out to Flossie, even then travelling the Long Trail and facing into the bitter North to meet a man who might not wait for her. A shrinking, clinging sort of a girl, Freda pictured her, with weak mouth and pretty pouting lips, blow-away sun-kissed hair, and eyes full of the merry shallows and the lesser joys of life. But she also pictured Flossie, face nose-strapped and frost-rimed, stumbling wearily behind the dogs. Wherefore she smiled, dancing one night, upon Floyd Vanderlip.

Few men are so constituted that they may receive the smile of Freda unmoved; nor among them can Floyd Vanderlip be accounted. The grace he had found with the model-woman had caused him to re-measure himself, and by the favor in which he now stood with the Greek dancer he felt himself doubly a man. There were unknown qualities and depths in him, evidently, which they perceived. He did not know exactly what those qualities and depths were, but he had a hazy idea that they were there somewhere, and of them was bred a great pride in himself. A man who could force two women such as these to look upon him a second time, was certainly a most remarkable man. Some day, when he had the time, he would sit down and analyze his strength; but now, just now, he would take what the gods had given him. And a thin little thought began to lift itself, and he fell to wondering whatever under the sun he had seen in Flossie, and to regret exceedingly that he had sent for her. Of course, Freda was out of the running. His dumps were the richest on Bonanza Creek, and they were many, while he was a man of responsibility and position. But Loraine Lisznayi—

she was just the woman. Her life had been large; she could do the honors of his establishment and give tone to his dollars.

But Freda smiled, and continued to smile, till he came to spend much time with her. When she, too, rode down the street behind his wolf-dogs, the model-woman found food for thought, and the next time they were together dazzled him with her princes and cardinals and personal little anecdotes of courts and kings. She also showed him dainty missives, superscribed, "My dear Loraine," and ended "Most affectionately yours," and signed by the given name of a real live queen on a throne. And he marvelled in his heart that the great woman should deign to waste so much as a moment upon him. But she played him cleverly, making flattering contrasts and comparisons between him and the noble phantoms she drew mainly from her fancy, till he went away dizzy with self-delight and sorrowing for the world which had been denied him so long. Freda was a more masterful woman. If she flattered, no one knew it. Should she stoop, the stoop were unobserved. If a man felt she thought well of him, so subtly was the feeling conveyed that he could not for the life of him say why or how. So she tightened her grip upon Floyd Vanderlip and rode daily behind his dogs.

And just here is where the mistake occurred. The buzz rose loudly and more definitely, coupled now with the name of the dancer, and Mrs. Eppingwell heard. She, too, thought of Flossie lifting her moccasined feet through the endless hours, and Floyd Vanderlip was invited up the hillside to tea, and invited often. This quite took his breath away, and he became drunken with appreciation of himself. Never was man so maltreated. His soul had become a thing for which three women struggled, while a fourth was on the way to claim it. And three such women!

But Mrs. Eppingwell and the mistake she made. She spoke of the affair, tentatively, to Sitka Charley, who had sold dogs to the Greek girl. But no names were mentioned. The nearest approach to it was when Mrs. Eppingwell said, "This—er—horrid woman," and Sitka Charley, with the model-woman strong in his thoughts, had echoed, "—er— horrid woman." And he agreed with her, that it was a wicked thing for a woman to come between a man and the girl he was to marry. "A mere girl, Charley," she said, "I am sure she is. And she is coming into a strange country without a friend when she gets here. We must do something." Sitka Charley promised his help, and went away thinking what a wicked woman this Loraine Lisznayi must be, also what noble women Mrs. Eppingwell and Freda were to interest themselves in the welfare of the unknown Flossie.

Now Mrs. Eppingwell was open as the day. To Sitka Charley, who took her once past the Hills of Silence, belongs the glory of having memorialized her clear-searching eyes, her clear-ringing voice, and her utter downright frankness. Her lips had a way of stiffening to command, and she was used to coming straight to the point. Having taken Floyd Vanderlip's measurement, she did not dare this with him; but she was not afraid to go down into the town to Freda. And down she went, in the bright light of day, to the house of the dancer. She was above silly tongues, as was her husband, the captain. She wished to see this woman and to speak with her, nor was she aware of any reason why she should not. So she stood in the snow at the Greek girl's door, with the frost at sixty below, and parleyed with the waiting-maid for a full five minutes. She had also the pleasure of being turned away from that door, and of going back up the hill, wroth at heart for the indignity which had been put upon her. "Who was this woman that she should refuse to see her?" she asked herself. One would think it the other way around, and she herself but a dancing girl denied at the door of the wife of a captain. As it was, she knew, had Freda come up the hill to her,—no matter what the errand,—she would have made her welcome at her fire, and they would have sat there as two women, and talked, merely as two women. She had overstepped convention and lowered herself, but she had thought it different with the women down in the town. And she was ashamed that she had laid herself open to such dishonor, and her thoughts of Freda were unkind.

Not that Freda deserved this. Mrs. Eppingwell had descended to meet her who was without caste, while she, strong in the traditions of her own earlier status, had not permitted it. She could worship such a woman, and she would have asked no greater joy than to have had her into the cabin and sat with her, just sat with her, for an hour. But her respect for Mrs. Eppingwell, and her respect for herself, who was beyond respect, had prevented her doing that which she most desired. Though not quite recovered from the recent visit of Mrs. McFee, the wife of the minister, who had descended upon her in a whirlwind of exhortation and brimstone, she could not imagine what had prompted the present visit. She was not aware of any particular wrong she had done, and surely this woman who waited at the door was not concerned with the welfare of her soul. Why had she come? For all the curiosity she could not help but feel, she steeled herself in the pride of those who are without pride, and trembled in the inner room like a maid on the first caress of a lover. If Mrs. Eppingwell suffered going up the hill, she too suffered, lying face downward on the bed, dry-eyed, dry-mouthed, dumb.

Mrs. Eppingwell's knowledge of human nature was great. She aimed at universality. She had found it easy to step from the civilized and contemplate things from the barbaric aspect. She could comprehend certain primal and analogous characteristics in a hungry wolf-dog or a starving man, and predicate lines of action to be pursued by either under like conditions. To her, a woman was a woman, whether garbed in purple or the rags of the gutter; Freda was a woman. She would not have been surprised had she been taken into the dancer's cabin and encountered on common ground; nor surprised had she been taken in and flaunted in prideless arrogance. But to be treated as she had been treated, was unexpected and disappointing. Ergo, she had not caught Freda's point of view. And this was good. There are some points of view which cannot be gained save through much travail and personal crucifixion, and it were well for the world that its Mrs. Eppingwells should, in certain ways, fall short of universality. One cannot understand defilement without laying hands to pitch, which is very sticky, while there be plenty willing to undertake the experiment. All of which is of small concern, beyond the fact that it gave Mrs. Eppingwell ground for grievance, and bred for her a greater love in the Greek girl's heart.

III

And in this way things went along for a month,—Mrs. Eppingwell striving to withhold the man from the Greek dancer's blandishments against the time of Flossie's coming; Flossie lessening the miles each day on the dreary trail; Freda pitting her strength against the model-woman; the model-woman straining every nerve to land the prize; and the man moving through it all like a flying shuttle, very proud of himself, whom he believed to be a second Don Juan.

It was nobody's fault except the man's that Loraine Lisznayi at last landed him. The way of a man with a maid may be too wonderful to know, but the way of a woman with a man passeth all conception; whence the prophet were indeed unwise who would dare forecast Floyd Vanderlip's course twenty-four hours in advance. Perhaps the model-woman's attraction lay in that to the eye she was a handsome animal; perhaps she fascinated him with her old-world talk of palaces and princes; leastwise she dazzled him whose life had been worked out in uncultured roughness, and he at last agreed to her suggestion of a run down the river and a marriage at Forty Mile. In token of his intention he bought dogs from Sitka Charley,—more than one sled is necessary when a woman like Loraine Lisznayi takes to the trail, and then went up the creek to give orders for the superintendence of his Bonanza mines during his absence.

He had given it out, rather vaguely, that he needed the animals for sledding lumber from the mill to his sluices, and right here is where Sitka Charley demonstrated his fitness.

He agreed to furnish dogs on a given date, but no sooner had Floyd Vanderlip turned his toes up-creek, than Charley hied himself away in perturbation to Loraine Lisznayi. Did she know where Mr. Vanderlip had gone? He had agreed to supply that gentleman with a big string of dogs by a certain time; but that shameless one, the German trader Meyers, had been buying up the brutes and skimped the market. It was very necessary he should see Mr. Vanderlip, because of the shameless one he would be all of a week behindhand in filling the contract. She did know where he had gone? Up-creek? Good! He would strike out after him at once and inform him of the unhappy delay. Did he understand her to say that Mr. Vanderlip needed the dogs on Friday night? that he must have them by that time? It was too bad, but it was the fault of the shameless one who had bid up the prices. They had jumped fifty dollars per head, and should he buy on the rising market he would lose by the contract. He wondered if Mr. Vanderlip would be willing to meet the advance. She knew he would? Being Mr. Vanderlip's friend, she would even meet the difference herself? And he was to say nothing about it? She was kind to so look to his interests. Friday night, did she say? Good! The dogs would be on hand.

An hour later, Freda knew the elopement was to be pulled off on Friday night; also, that Floyd Vanderlip had gone up-creek, and her hands were tied. On Friday morning, Devereaux, the official courier, bearing despatches from the Governor, arrived over the ice. Besides the despatches, he brought news of Flossie. He had passed her camp at Sixty Mile; humans and dogs were in good condition; and she would doubtless be in on the morrow. Mrs. Eppingwell experienced a great relief on hearing this; Floyd Vanderlip was safe up-creek, and ere the Greek girl could again lay hands upon him, his bride would be on the ground. But that afternoon her big St. Bernard, valiantly defending her front stoop, was downed by a foraging party of trail-starved Malemutes. He was buried beneath the hirsute mass for about thirty seconds, when rescued by a couple of axes and as many stout men. Had he remained down two minutes, the chances were large that he would have been roughly apportioned and carried away in the respective bellies of the attacking party; but as it was, it was a mere case of neat and expeditious mangling. Sitka Charley came to repair the damages, especially a right fore-paw which had inadvertently been left a fraction of a second too long in some other dog's mouth. As he put on his mittens to go, the talk turned upon Flossie and in natural sequence passed on to the—"er horrid woman." Sitka Charley remarked incidentally that she intended jumping out down river that night with Floyd Vanderlip, and further ventured the information that accidents were very likely at that time of year.

So Mrs. Eppingwell's thoughts of Freda were unkinder than ever. She wrote a note, addressed it to the man in question, and intrusted it to a messenger who lay in wait at the mouth of Bonanza Creek. Another man, bearing a note from Freda, also waited at that strategic point. So it happened that Floyd Vanderlip, riding his sled merrily down with the last daylight, received the notes together. He tore Freda's across. No, he would not go to see her. There were greater things afoot that night. Besides, she was out of the running. But Mrs. Eppingwell! He would observe her last wish,—or rather, the last wish it would be possible for him to observe,—and meet her at the Governor's ball to hear what she had to say. From the tone of the writing it was evidently important; perhaps— He smiled fondly, but failed to shape the thought. Confound it all, what a lucky fellow he was with the women any way! Scattering her letter to the frost, he *mushed* the dogs into a swinging lope and headed for his cabin. It was to be a masquerade, and he had to dig up the costume used at the Opera House a couple of months before. Also, he had to shave and to eat. Thus it was that he, alone of all interested, was unaware of Flossie's proximity.

"Have them down to the water-hole off the hospital, at midnight, sharp. Don't fail me," he said to Sitka Charley, who dropped in with the advice that only one dog was lacking to fill the bill, and that that one would be forthcoming in an hour or so. "Here's the sack. There's the scales. Weigh out your own dust and don't bother me. I've got to get ready for the ball."

Sitka Charley weighed out his pay and departed, carrying with him a letter to Loraine Lisznayi, the contents of which he correctly imagined to refer to a meeting at the water-hole of the hospital, at midnight, sharp.

IV

Twice Freda sent messengers up to the Barracks, where the dance was in full swing, and as often they came back without answers. Then she did what only Freda could do—put on her furs, masked her face, and went up herself to the Governor's ball. Now there happened to be a custom—not an original one by any means—to which the official clique had long since become addicted. It was a very wise custom, for it furnished protection to the womankind of the officials and gave greater selectness to their revels. Whenever a masquerade was given, a committee was chosen, the sole function of which was to stand by the door and peep beneath each and every mask. Most men did not clamor to be placed upon this committee, while the very ones who least desired the honor were the ones whose services were most required. The chaplain was not well enough acquainted with the faces and places of the townspeople to know whom to admit and whom to turn away. In like condition were the several other worthy gentlemen who would have asked nothing better than to so serve. To fill the coveted place, Mrs. McFee would have risked her chance of salvation, and did, one night, when a certain trio passed in under her guns and muddled things considerably before their identity was discovered. Thereafter only the fit were chosen, and very ungracefully did they respond.

On this particular night Prince was at the door. Pressure had been brought to bear, and he had not yet recovered from amaze at his having consented to undertake a task which bid fair to lose him half his friends, merely for the sake of pleasing the other half. Three or four of the men he had

146

refused were men whom he had known on creek and trail,—good comrades, but not exactly eligible for so select an affair. He was canvassing the expediency of resigning the post there and then, when a woman tripped in under the light. Freda! He could swear it by the furs, did he not know that poise of head so well. The last one to expect in all the world. He had given her better judgment than to thus venture the ignominy of refusal, or, if she passed, the scorn of women. He shook his head, without scrutiny; he knew her too well to be mistaken. But she pressed closer. She lifted the black silk ribbon and as quickly lowered it again. For one flashing, eternal second he looked upon her face. It was not for nothing, the saying which had arisen in the country, that Freda played with men as a child with bubbles. Not a word was spoken. Prince stepped aside, and a few moments later might have been seen resigning, with warm incoherence, the post to which he had been unfaithful.

* * * * *

A woman, flexible of form, slender, yet rhythmic of strength in every movement, now pausing with this group, now scanning that, urged a restless and devious course among the revellers. Men recognized the furs, and marvelled,—men who should have served upon the door committee; but they were not prone to speech. Not so with the women. They had better eyes for the lines of figure and tricks of carriage, and they knew this form to be one with which they were unfamiliar; likewise the furs. Mrs. McFee, emerging from the supper-room where all was in readiness, caught one flash of the blazing, questing eyes through the silken mask-slits, and received a start. She tried to recollect where she had seen the like, and a vivid picture was recalled of a certain proud and rebellious sinner whom she had once encountered on a fruitless errand for the Lord.

So it was that the good woman took the trail in hot and righteous wrath, a trail which brought her ultimately into the company of Mrs. Eppingwell and Floyd Vanderlip. Mrs. Eppingwell had just found the opportunity to talk with the

147

man. She had determined, now that Flossie was so near at hand, to proceed directly to the point, and an incisive little ethical discourse was titillating on the end of her tongue, when the couple became three. She noted, and pleasurably, the faintly foreign accent of the "Beg pardon" with which the furred woman prefaced her immediate appropriation of Floyd Vanderlip; and she courteously bowed her permission for them to draw a little apart.

Then it was that Mrs. McFee's righteous hand descended, and accompanying it in its descent was a black mask torn from a startled woman. A wonderful face and brilliant eyes were exposed to the quiet curiosity of those who looked that way, and they were everybody. Floyd Vanderlip was rather confused. The situation demanded instant action on the part of a man who was not beyond his depth, while *he* hardly knew where he was. He stared helplessly about him. Mrs. Eppingwell was perplexed. She could not comprehend. An explanation was forthcoming, somewhere, and Mrs. McFee was equal to it.

"Mrs. Eppingwell," and her Celtic voice rose shrilly, "it is with great pleasure I make you acquainted with Freda Moloof, *Miss* Freda Moloof, as I understand."

Freda involuntarily turned. With her own face bared, she felt as in a dream, naked, upon her turned the clothed features and gleaming eyes of the masked circle. It seemed, almost, as though a hungry wolf-pack girdled her, ready to drag her down. It might chance that some felt pity for her, she thought, and at the thought, hardened. She would by far prefer their scorn. Strong of heart was she, this woman, and though she had hunted the prey into the midst of the pack, Mrs. Eppingwell or no Mrs. Eppingwell, she could not forego the kill.

But here Mrs. Eppingwell did a strange thing. So this, at last, was Freda, she mused, the dancer and the destroyer of men; the woman from whose door she had been turned. And she, too, felt the imperious creature's nakedness as though it were her own. Perhaps it was this, her Saxon disinclination to meet a disadvantaged foe, perhaps, forsooth, that it might give her greater strength in the struggle for the man, and it might have been a little of both; but be that as it may, she did do this strange thing. When Mrs. McFee's thin voice, vibrant with malice, had raised, and Freda turned involuntarily, Mrs. Eppingwell also turned, removed her mask, and inclined her head in acknowledgment.

It was another flashing, eternal second, during which these two women regarded each other. The one, eyes blazing, meteoric; at bay, aggressive; suffering in advance and resenting in advance the scorn and ridicule and insult she had thrown herself open to; a beautiful, burning, bubbling lava cone of flesh and spirit. And the other, calm-eyed, cool-browed, serene; strong in her own integrity, with faith in herself, thoroughly at ease; dispassionate, imperturbable; a figure chiselled from some cold marble quarry. Whatever gulf there might exist, she recognized it not. No bridging, no descending; her attitude was that of perfect equality. She stood tranquilly on the ground of their common womanhood. And this maddened Freda. Not so, had she been of lesser breed; but her soul's plummet knew not the bottomless, and she could follow the other into the deeps of her deepest depths and read her aright. "Why do you not draw back your garment's hem?" she was fain to cry out, all in that flashing, dazzling second. "Spit upon me, revile me, and it were greater mercy than this!" She trembled. Her nostrils distended and quivered. But she drew herself in check, returned the inclination of head, and turned to the man.

"Come with me, Floyd," she said simply. "I want you now."

"What the—" he began explosively, and quit as suddenly, discreet enough to not round it off. Where the deuce had his wits gone, anyway? Was ever a man more foolishly placed? He gurgled deep down in his throat and high up in the roof of his mouth, heaved as one his big shoulders and his indecision, and glared appealingly at the two women.

"I beg pardon, just a moment, but may I speak first with Mr. Vanderlip?" Mrs. Eppingwell's voice, though flute-like and low, predicated will in its every cadence.

The man looked his gratitude. He, at least, was willing enough.

"I'm very sorry," from Freda. "There isn't time. He must come at once." The conventional phrases dropped easily from her lips, but she could not forbear to smile inwardly at their inadequacy and weakness. She would much rather have shrieked.

"But, Miss Moloof, who are you that you may possess yourself of Mr. Vanderlip and command his actions?"

Whereupon relief brightened his face, and the man beamed his approval. Trust Mrs. Eppingwell to drag him clear. Freda had met her match this time.

"I—I—" Freda hesitated, and then her feminine mind putting on its harness—"and who are you to ask this question?"

"I? I am Mrs. Eppingwell, and—"

"There!" the other broke in sharply. "You are the wife of a captain, who is therefore your husband. I am only a dancing girl. What do you with this man?"

"Such unprecedented behavior!" Mrs. McFee ruffled herself and cleared for action, but Mrs. Eppingwell shut her mouth with a look and developed a new attack.

"Since Miss Moloof appears to hold claims upon you, Mr. Vanderlip, and is in too great haste to grant me a few seconds of your time, I am forced to appeal directly to you. May I speak with you, alone, and now?"

Mrs. McFee's jaws brought together with a snap. That settled the disgraceful situation.

"Why, er—that is, certainly," the man stammered. "Of course, of course," growing more effusive at the prospect of deliverance.

Men are only gregarious vertebrates, domesticated and evolved, and the chances are large that it was because the Greek girl had in her time dealt with wilder masculine beasts of the human sort; for she turned upon the man with hell's tides aflood in her blazing eyes, much as a bespangled lady upon a lion which has suddenly imbibed the pernicious theory that he is a free agent. The beast in him fawned to the lash.

"That is to say, ah, afterward. To-morrow, Mrs. Eppingwell; yes, to-morrow. That is what I meant." He solaced himself with the fact, should he remain, that more embarrassment awaited. Also, he had an engagement which he must keep shortly, down by the water-hole off the hospital. Ye gods! he had never given Freda credit! Wasn't she magnificent!

"I'll thank you for my mask, Mrs. McFee."

That lady, for the nonce speechless, turned over the article in question.

"Good-night, Miss Moloof." Mrs. Eppingwell was royal even in defeat.

Freda reciprocated, though barely downing the impulse to clasp the other's knees and beg forgiveness,—no, not forgiveness, but something, she knew not what, but which she none the less greatly desired.

The man was for her taking his arm; but she had made her kill in the midst of the pack, and that which led kings to drag their vanquished at the chariot-tail, led her toward the door alone, Floyd Vanderlip close at heel and striving to re-establish his mental equilibrium.

V

It was bitter cold. As the trail wound, a quarter of a mile brought them to the dancer's cabin, by which time her moist breath had coated her face frostily, while his had massed his heavy mustache till conversation was painful. By the greenish light of the aurora borealis, the quicksilver showed itself frozen hard in the bulb of the thermometer which hung outside the door. A thousand dogs, in pitiful chorus, wailed their ancient wrongs and claimed mercy from the unheeding stars. Not a breath of air was moving. For them there was no shelter from the cold, no shrewd crawling to leeward in snug nooks. The frost was everywhere, and they lay in the open, ever and anon stretching their trail-stiffened muscles and lifting the long wolf-howl.

They did not talk at first, the man and the woman. While the maid helped Freda off with her wraps, Floyd Vanderlip replenished the fire; and by the time the maid had withdrawn to an inner room, his head over the stove, he was busily thawing out his burdened upper lip. After that he rolled a cigarette and watched her lazily through the fragrant eddies. She stole a glance at the clock. It lacked half an hour of midnight. How was she to hold him? Was he angry for that which she had done? What was his mood? What mood of hers could meet his best? Not that she doubted herself. No, no. Hold him she could, if need be at pistol point, till Sitka Charley's work was done, and Devereaux's too.

There were many ways, and with her knowledge of this her contempt for the man increased. As she leaned her head on her hand, a fleeting vision of her own girlhood, with its mournful climacteric and tragic ebb, was vouchsafed her, and for the moment she was minded to read him a lesson from it. God! it must be less than human brute who could not be held by such a tale, told as she could tell it, but— bah! He was not worth it, nor worth the pain to her. The candle was positioned just right, and even as she thought of these things sacredly shameful to her, he was pleasuring in the transparent pinkiness of her ear. She noted his eye, took the cue, and turned her head till the clean profile of the face was presented. Not the least was that profile among her virtues. She could not help the lines upon which she had been builded, and they were very good; but she had long since learned those lines, and though little they needed, was not above advantaging them to the best of her ability. The candle began to flicker. She could not do anything ungracefully, but that did not prevent her improving upon nature a bit, when she reached forth and deftly snuffed the red wick from the midst of the yellow flame. Again she rested head on hand, this time regarding the man thoughtfully, and any man is pleased when thus regarded by a pretty woman.

She was in little haste to begin. If dalliance were to his liking, it was to hers. To him it was very comfortable, soothing his lungs with nicotine and gazing upon her. It was snug and warm here, while down by the water-hole began a trail which he would soon be hitting through the chilly hours. He felt he ought to be angry with Freda for the scene she had created, but somehow he didn't feel a bit wrathful. Like as not there wouldn't have been any scene if it hadn't been for that McFee woman. If he were the Governor, he would put a poll tax of a hundred ounces a quarter upon her and her kind and all gospel sharks and sky pilots. And certainly Freda had behaved very ladylike, held her own with Mrs. Eppingwell besides. Never gave the girl credit for the grit. He looked lingeringly over her, coming back now and again to the eyes, behind the deep earnestness of which he could not guess lay concealed a deeper sneer. And, Jove, wasn't she well put up! Wonder why she looked at him so? Did she want to marry him, too? Like as not; but she wasn't the only one. Her looks were in her favor, weren't they? And young—younger than Loraine Lisznayi. She couldn't be more than twenty-three or four, twenty-five at most. And she'd never get stout. Anybody could guess that the first time. He couldn't say it of Loraine, though. *She* certainly had put on flesh since the day she served as model. Huh! once he got her on trail he'd take it off. Put her on the snowshoes to break ahead of the dogs. Never knew it to fail, yet. But his thought leaped ahead to the palace under the lazy Mediterranean sky—and how would it be with Loraine then? No frost, no trail, no famine now and again to cheer the monotony, and she getting older and piling it on with every sunrise. While this girl Freda—he sighed his unconscious regret that he had missed being born under the flag of the Turk, and came back to Alaska.

"Well?" Both hands of the clock pointed perpendicularly to midnight, and it was high time he was getting down to the water-hole.

"Oh!" Freda started, and she did it prettily, delighting him as his fellows have ever been delighted by their womankind. When a man is made to believe that a woman, looking upon him thoughtfully, has lost herself in meditation over him, that man needs be an extremely cold-blooded individual in order to trim his sheets, set a lookout, and steer clear.

"I was just wondering what you wanted to see me about," he explained, drawing his chair up to hers by the table.

"Floyd," she looked him steadily in the eyes, "I am tired of the whole business. I want to go away. I can't live it out here till the river breaks. If I try, I'll die. I am sure of it. I want to quit it all and go away, and I want to do it at once."

She laid her hand in mute appeal upon the back of his, which turned over and became a prison. Another one, he thought, just throwing herself at him. Guess it wouldn't hurt Loraine to cool her feet by the water-hole a little longer.

"Well?" This time from Freda, but softly and anxiously.

"I don't know what to say," he hastened to answer, adding to himself that it was coming along quicker than he had expected. "Nothing I'd like better, Freda. You know that well enough." He pressed her hand, palm to palm. She nodded. Could she wonder that she despised the breed?

"But you see, I—I'm engaged. Of course you know that. And the girl's coming into the country to marry me. Don't know what was up with me when I asked her, but it was a long while back, and I was all-fired young—"

"I want to go away, out of the land, anywhere," she went on, disregarding the obstacle he had reared up and apologized for. "I have been running over the men I know and reached the conclusion that—that—"

"I was the likeliest of the lot?"

She smiled her gratitude for his having saved her the embarrassment of confession. He drew her head against his shoulder with the free hand, and somehow the scent of her hair got into his nostrils. Then he discovered that a common pulse throbbed, throbbed, throbbed, where their palms were in contact. This phenomenon is easily comprehensible from a physiological standpoint, but to the man who makes the discovery for the first time, it is a most wonderful thing. Floyd Vanderlip had caressed more shovel-handles than women's hands in his time, so this was an experience quite new and delightfully strange. And when Freda turned her head against his shoulder, her hair brushing his cheek till his eyes met hers, full and at close range, luminously soft, ay, and tender—why, whose fault was it that he lost his grip utterly? False to Flossie, why not to Loraine? Even if the women did keep bothering him, that was no reason he should make up his mind in a hurry. Why, he had slathers of money, and Freda was just the girl to grace it. A wife she'd make him for other men to envy. But go slow. He must be cautious.

"You don't happen to care for palaces, do you?" he asked.

She shook her head.

"Well, I had a hankering after them myself, till I got to thinking, a while back, and I've about sized it up that one'd get fat living in palaces, and soft and lazy."

155

"Yes, it's nice for a time, but you soon grow tired of it, I imagine," she hastened to reassure him. "The world is good, but life should be many-sided. Rough and knock about for a while, and then rest up somewhere. Off to the South Seas on a yacht, then a nibble of Paris; a winter in South America and a summer in Norway; a few months in England—"

"Good society?"

"Most certainly—the best; and then, heigho! for the dogs and sleds and the Hudson Bay Country. Change, you know. A strong man like you, full of vitality and go, could not possibly stand a palace for a year. It is all very well for effeminate men, but you weren't made for such a life. You are masculine, intensely masculine."

"Think so?"

"It does not require thinking. I know. Have you ever noticed that it was easy to make women care for you?"

His dubious innocence was superb.

"It is very easy. And why? Because you are masculine. You strike the deepest chords of a woman's heart. You are something to cling to,—big-muscled, strong, and brave. In short, because you *are* a man."

She shot a glance at the clock. It was half after the hour. She had given a margin of thirty minutes to Sitka Charley; and it did not matter, now, when Devereaux arrived. Her work was done. She lifted her head, laughed her genuine mirth, slipped her hand clear, and rising to her feet called the maid.

"Alice, help Mr. Vanderlip on with his *parka*. His mittens are on the sill by the stove."

The man could not understand.

"Let me thank you for your kindness, Floyd. Your time was invaluable to me, and it was indeed good of you. The turning to the left, as you leave the cabin, leads the quickest to the water-hole. Good-night. I am going to bed."

Floyd Vanderlip employed strong words to express his perplexity and disappointment. Alice did not like to hear men swear, so dropped his *parka* on the floor and tossed his mittens on top of it. Then he made a break for Freda, and she ruined her retreat to the inner room by tripping over the *parka*. He brought her up standing with a rude grip on the wrist. But she only laughed. She was not afraid of men. Had they not wrought their worst with her, and did she not still endure?

"Don't be rough," she said finally. "On second thought," here she looked at his detaining hand, "I've decided not to go to bed yet a while. Do sit down and be comfortable instead of ridiculous. Any questions?"

"Yes, my lady, and reckoning, too." He still kept his hold. "What do you know about the water-hole? What did you mean by—no, never mind. One question at a time."

"Oh, nothing much. Sitka Charley had an appointment there with somebody you may know, and not being anxious for a man of your known charm to be present, fell back upon me to kindly help him. That's all. They're off now, and a good half hour ago."

"Where? Down river and without me? And he an Indian!"

"There's no accounting for taste, you know, especially in a woman."

"But how do I stand in this deal? I've lost four thousand dollars' worth of dogs and a tidy bit of a woman, and nothing to show for it. Except you," he added as an afterthought, "and cheap you are at the price."

157

Freda shrugged her shoulders.

"You might as well get ready. I'm going out to borrow a couple of teams of dogs, and we'll start in as many hours."

"I am very sorry, but I'm going to bed."

"You'll pack if you know what's good for you. Go to bed, or not, when I get my dogs outside, so help me, onto the sled you go. Mebbe you fooled with me, but I'll just see your bluff and take you in earnest. Hear me?"

He closed on her wrist till it hurt, but on her lips a smile was growing, and she seemed to listen intently to some outside sound. There was a jingle of dog bells, and a man's voice crying "Haw!" as a sled took the turning and drew up at the cabin.

"*Now* will you let me go to bed?"

As Freda spoke she threw open the door. Into the warm room rushed the frost, and on the threshold, garbed in trail-worn furs, knee-deep in the swirling vapor, against a background of flaming borealis, a woman hesitated. She removed her nose-trap and stood blinking blindly in the white candlelight. Floyd Vanderlip stumbled forward.

"Floyd!" she cried, relieved and glad, and met him with a tired bound.

What could he but kiss the armful of furs? And a pretty armful it was, nestling against him wearily, but happy.

"It was good of you," spoke the armful, "to send Mr. Devereaux with fresh dogs after me, else I would not have been in till to-morrow."

The man looked blankly across at Freda, then the light breaking in upon him, "And wasn't it good of Devereaux to go?"

158

"Couldn't wait a bit longer, could you, dear?" Flossie snuggled closer.

"Well, I was getting sort of impatient," he confessed glibly, at the same time drawing her up till her feet left the floor, and getting outside the door.

That same night an inexplicable thing happened to the Reverend James Brown, missionary, who lived among the natives several miles down the Yukon and saw to it that the trails they trod led to the white man's paradise. He was roused from his sleep by a strange Indian, who gave into his charge not only the soul but the body of a woman, and having done this drove quickly away. This woman was heavy, and handsome, and angry, and in her wrath unclean words fell from her mouth. This shocked the worthy man, but he was yet young and her presence would have been pernicious (in the simple eyes of his flock), had she not struck out on foot for Dawson with the first gray of dawn.

The shock to Dawson came many days later, when the summer had come and the population honored a certain royal lady at Windsor by lining the Yukon's bank and watching Sitka Charley rise up with flashing paddle and drive the first canoe across the line. On this day of the races, Mrs. Eppingwell, who had learned and unlearned numerous things, saw Freda for the first time since the night of the ball. "Publicly, mind you," as Mrs. McFee expressed it, "without regard or respect for the morals of the community," she went up to the dancer and held out her hand. At first, it is remembered by those who saw, the girl shrank back, then words passed between the two, and Freda, great Freda, broke down and wept on the shoulder of the captain's wife. It was not given to Dawson to know why Mrs. Eppingwell should crave forgiveness of a Greek dancing girl, but she did it publicly, and it was unseemly.

It were well not to forget Mrs. McFee. She took a cabin passage on the first steamer going out. She also took with her a theory which she had achieved in the silent watches of the long dark nights; and it is her conviction that the Northland is unregenerate because it is so cold there. Fear of hell-fire cannot be bred in an ice-box. This may appear dogmatic, but it is Mrs. McFee's theory.

www.ingramcontent.com/pod-product-compliance
Lightning Source LLC
Chambersburg PA
CBHW030229180626
46810CB00008B/3037